THE GHOST THAT CAME ALIVE

THE GHOST THAT CAME ALIVE

by Vic Crume

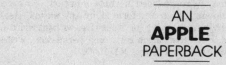

AN
APPLE
PAPERBACK

SCHOLASTIC INC.
New York Toronto London Auckland Sydney

ISBN 0-590-46147-8

12 11 10 9 8 7 6 5 4 3 2 1   10   2 3 4 5 6 7/9

Printed in the U.S.A.   28

1

By the time Jenny Blair stepped out on the cottage porch where the family was having breakfast, Jenny's twin brother, Chris, was eating his third blueberry muffin, and small Tommy was reaching for his fourth.

"Good morning!" their father, Dr. Blair, called out cheerfully. "You fooled me, Jenny. I thought you'd be the first one up on going-home day."

Jenny sighed. "Good morning. I thought I would, too, but . . ." She sat down and sighed again.

"What's the matter, dear?" Mrs. Blair asked. "Don't you feel well?"

"Oh, I'm all right — I guess," Jenny replied slowly. "But I had awful dreams last night."

Nobody bothered to ask what the dreams were, and Jenny looked around at her family: her energetic, ex-nurse mother and doctor father, five-year-old Tommy, and big brother Jim — he and Emily, Jenny's pretty, dark-haired sister, were

1

both in high school. Last of all, she glanced at Chris, who grinned back mockingly.

Everybody looks as though blueberry muffins were the only thing they had to worry about, Jenny thought. But what she said was, "You know, it's really funny."

"What's really funny?" her father asked. "You don't look as though you thought *anything* was funny this morning."

Jenny pushed her long brown hair behind her ears. "Well, it's funny that I'm the only one in the family who ever has a *premonition*."

"Premonition, dear?" asked Mrs. Blair.

Jenny nodded. "Yes. A premonition of *doom*. A feeling something dreadful is going to happen."

Chris burst out laughing. "Pay no attention, Mom," he said. "You know, Jenny has one every year — the day we close the cottage and leave for home."

Jenny eyed him coldly, then helped herself to a muffin. Munching, she stared out across the little inlet that led to the blue Atlantic in the distance. She started to say that her premonition was more than going-home blues, then decided not to. "The important thing," she said finally, "is that this family is always leaving the shore when everyone else is just arriving. We're always going in the wrong direction on Labor Day weekends."

Mrs. Blair smiled. "Now Jenny, you know how your father feels about holiday traffic. Besides, I should think that with a thirteenth birthday coming up, you and Chris would like to be home with your old friends."

"Sure, Jenny." Jim grinned. "It isn't just any birthday when a person gets to be a teenager."

"That's another sad thing," said Jenny gloomily. "Here I am, saying good-bye to everything here, all the time knowing that just next week I face my *thirteenth* year — unlucky 13 — and that I'll have to say good-bye to my — my childhood."

"Oh for — " Chris pulled back his chair. "Excuse me, Mom? Personally, I can't stand this type of conversation. I think I'll go over and say good-bye to the Smith kids."

Jenny suddenly grinned. "Go ahead, Chris. I'll catch up with you."

"Take Tommy along with you, Chris," Mrs. Blair said, starting to clear the table. "Emily, would you strip the beds and put the laundry bag in the station wagon? Meantime, Jim, you could help your father with the breakfast dishes while I finish packing."

Dr. Blair looked up. "I don't suppose you'd let Jim and me out of KP duty to run over to the marina? I left the binoculars on the boat and there's no point in leaving them in dry dock for the winter. I thought Jim and I could drive over there in the small car while you and the girls packed the station wagon."

Mrs. Blair gave him a long steady look, but her

3

eyes twinkled. "What? Lose my dishwashing crew to pick up one pair of binoculars? No, dear. Not a chance."

With young Tommy bouncing in the lead, Chris and Jenny walked back down the path from the Smith cottage.

"Honestly, that child embarrasses me," Jenny said. "I'll bet Mrs. Smith thinks we don't feed him at home. Three slices of bacon and almost half a melon — and he'd just finished one breakfast."

"Well, he's a growing child," Chris replied.

"He'll be a growing-fat child if we don't watch him." Jenny frowned. "What'll we do next?"

"Keep on saying good-bye, I suppose." Chris grinned. "How about saying good-bye to the ocean?"

"Okay," Jenny agreed. "Come on, Tom," she called. "Not that way. We're going to the beach."

"Hey! Look at those thunderheads piling up!" Chris exclaimed. He pointed toward the ocean. "We're going to miss a big storm, I bet."

Jenny said gloomily, "And I just love storms."

"Cheer up," her twin replied. "Maybe it will follow us all the way home, and you can be in it for *hours*."

"It's a good thing, Jim, that you and Emily are driving back in the small car," Mrs. Blair said. "I don't know how we could wedge one more thing in this wagon."

Jim laughed. "Since when are Emily and I 'things,' Mom? I always — "

"You know what I meant, dear," his mother replied. "Now see if you can tuck these tennis rackets in someplace. And let's hurry. Look at that sky over in the east. I'd just as soon miss the storm, although Jenny . . ."

"Mother! Dad!" The porch door slammed and Chris came pounding into the cottage. "Come quick!" he cried. "It's Tommy. Something's awfully wrong with him. He's all doubled over."

Dr. Blair, on his way downstairs, hurried over to Chris. "Where is Tom?" he asked. His voice was calm but he was reaching for his medical bag.

"About halfway down the inlet path," Chris panted. "It happened all of a sudden. Jenny's with him. I think it's because he ate a second breakfast over at the Smiths'. We couldn't stop him and Jenny said — "

But his father was already half-striding, half-running down the inlet path.

In the next half hour, things happened fast. Dr. Blair and Mrs. Blair, in the small car, rushed Tommy off to the hospital in nearby Centertown.

"We'll call you from the hospital, kids," Dr. Blair said as they left.

5

Jenny, head bent and tears falling, stumbled back toward the cottage when the small car had disappeared down the lane.

Chris caught up with her. "For gosh sakes, Jenny, stop bawling. It isn't your fault that Tommy is a — a pig."

Jenny broke into a loud sob. "Pig!" she exclaimed. "How can you call our baby brother a *pig*?"

"Because he is," Chris answered calmly. "He's probably just got a bellyache."

"I prefer to say *stomach*ache," Jenny replied, mopping her tears. "And besides, being a doctor's child, I recognize appendicitis when I see it."

"Oh," Chris said. "Well, I'm a doctor's child, too — and I say it's just a bellyache. You know, Jenny — you're something. Really something."

But in his heart Chris knew Jenny might be right.

When the call came from the hospital, Jim answered the phone. Dr. Blair's voice was tense. "Burst appendix. Your mother is taking it pretty hard, Jim."

Everybody listened, trying to guess from Jim's words what the conversation might be. "Sure. Of course. Don't worry. Sure. Well, okay. What number should we call?" He motioned to Emily to jot down the number as he repeated it. "Okay. Tonight, then. Good-bye."

Jim turned to the others and ran his fingers through his brown hair. "Now, let me get it all lined up." He frowned. "Well, 1-2-3 — it goes like this: First — Dad said he and Mother are taking a room near the hospital and he wants us to call him from wherever we stop for the night."

"Stop for the night!" Emily exploded. "But why not stay here? I'd like to be somewhere near Tommy. What did he say about *him*?"

Jim shook his head. "I don't believe he knows yet. He just said that Mother would feel better if things went along as planned — except that I'll drive the wagon. I guess it's pretty sensible. That way Mom can sort of concentrate on Tommy.

"He's put me in charge. We'll lock up, and Dad will come back here to close the shutters before they leave for home. He wants us to stop by the hospital for money. He said to make it about noon. Tommy will be out of surgery by then and he'll have news for us."

Jim thought a minute. "I guess we'd better go by the marina and pick up the binoculars," he said. "We can do that on our way to the hospital. Dad wanted them."

Emily glanced at her watch. "Then let's get started. We haven't much time."

"It'll take just a second to get those binoculars," Jim said as he parked the big Blair wagon at the marina boat shed.

"I want to come, too," Chris cried, scrambling out.

"So do I," Jenny said, beginning to climb after him.

"Jenny, sit down." Emily turned around and pushed her younger sister back onto the seat.

"But I might have seen something that the boys would completely overlook," said Jenny, feeling hurt.

But Chris wasn't overlooking anything on the boat.

"Shouldn't we take this?" he asked Jim. He held out a metal box that held the signal flare pistol Dr. Blair always kept aboard.

Jim hesitated, then held out his hand. "Okay. Might as well. We can tuck it in somewhere, I guess."

"Would we get arrested for carrying a concealed weapon?"

"This isn't a weapon," Jim answered. "It's a very useful thing in case you're lost at sea. You can always hope somebody will see the flare light up and know you're in trouble."

"I've never seen it work," Chris said sadly.

"Lucky you. Come on. Let's go."

As the boys left the darkened boat shed, Chris pointed to the sky. "That's going to be some storm. Looks as though it's spreading all the way from here to Maine."

"Well, don't point that out to Mom when we

reach the hospital," Jim replied. "She's not like Jenny about storms, you know."

Chris scowled angrily. "Listen, Jim — I know you're in charge and everything. But I hope you're not turning into — an elder statesman, or somebody like that. As though I'd worry Mom. Wow!"

Jim's dark brows shot up, then he grinned. "Elder statesman? Hmm. That sounds pretty heavy. But I guess I know what you mean. Okay, I'll watch it!"

"Okay then." Chris fell into step beside his older brother.

But before the day was to end, Chris Blair was going to wish that Jim *was* an elder statesman — or that their dependable father was in charge.

2

Jim Blair's hands clenched the steering wheel as the heavy wagon swished along through a flooding downpour of wind-driven rain.

In the gathering dark, Emily, who was sitting beside Jim in front, turned on a small pocket flashlight to study the road map she had spread out on her lap. "It was that detour," she explained. "It wasn't shown on the map. I guess we should have stuck to the interstate highway. I thought this road would be shorter, but we're still a good thirty miles from Alston. That's the first town of any size we'll come to, but there ought to be plenty of motels there."

"Thirty miles more!" exclaimed Jenny.

"We'll starve!" said Chris.

Emily leaned forward. "They have a point, Jim. In this kind of a storm, I think we ought to begin looking for a motel now."

Jim peered ahead past the dizzying sweep of the windshield wipers. "You look for a motel," he

10

said grimly. "I'll just keep on looking for the road."

"That's the main thing — looking for the road," Chris called out. "If you ask me, we don't seem to be on it."

Just then, the right wheel dipped downward, and for a moment the big wagon lurched sickeningly to the right — toward the seaside, where a thunderous ocean was pounding the base of the cliffs.

Jenny slid into her twin's shoulder. "See?" Chris said disgustedly. "If you'd had your seat belt fastened, you wouldn't be smashing all over me." Then he went skidding into Jenny as the wagon narrowly missed a ditch along the left side of the road.

"Fasten your own seat belt," Jenny said, buckling hers.

"Kids, please!" Emily exclaimed. "You've — " She stopped in midsentence. "Whoa! Jim, I think we just passed a motel sign — I *think*."

As Jim carefully slowed and backed, sheets of water churned up. "I think this road's about to flood out," he said anxiously.

Cautiously he backed the wagon until the headlights shone on the sign Emily had glimpsed: DON'T LITTER.

"Don't litter!" Chris exclaimed in disgust. "Well, I suppose that means we can't throw Emily out."

Jim chuckled and eased the car forward. "What

11

this bunch needs is food. Hey! Look! Do I see lights ahead? I sure do."

It wasn't a motel, but it was a brightly lighted gas station with a roof over the pumps, and when the wagon nosed in off the highway, the travelers felt as though they had finally reached civilization again.

Of course it had been only several hours, but it seemed a long time since they'd left the hospital.

"Thank goodness you've got good sense and can take charge of things," Dr. Blair had said to Jim. "Tommy's going to be all right. But I think I'll stay on for a day or so to keep your mother company."

Now, as Jim turned off the engine, he was secretly doubting just how much good sense he had shown. "I guess I should have pulled into some motel earlier, when I saw that sky up ahead getting purple-black," he said to himself.

He rolled down the window as the station attendant came toward the car. "Fill it up, please," he said. Then he climbed out from behind the wheel to stretch his legs a bit. The others scattered off to the rest rooms.

"Any motels between here and Alston?" Jim asked the attendant.

"There're a couple not more than five miles up the road," came the answer. "They're not too great. Don't get much business since the new highway cut them off from the heavy traffic. But then — any old port in a storm, I guess."

Jim grinned. "You're sure right. Is one any better than the other?"

"Don't know. Never stayed at either. The first one's called the Sea Cove Inn. But the next one — that's the one called Cliffside — has a restaurant."

"That's for us, then. Have you had any report on the weather? We seem to be traveling right along with this storm."

The attendant shook his head. "Going to get worse before it gets better. They predicted a big electrical storm. So far, we've had only wind and rain. Much more water and this road is sure going to flood out between here and Alston."

"I hope not. How much do we owe you?" Jim asked.

While he paid the bill, Emily came running back to the car. "I've called the hospital and I spoke with Mom. Tommy's getting along fine, but Mom said to call tomorrow before we start out. She said Dad wants to explain several dozen things he wants you to do — like getting the phone connected, and that kind of stuff. I told her we'd be stopping in Alston tonight."

Jim put away his wallet. "Want the latest bulletin? We're going on up the road about five miles where there's a motel and restaurant. How does that sound?"

"Great!"

"Great, if the road holds up," Jim added gloomily.

The road was still there but only just. And hardly was the wagon back on it when the rain came down even harder than before, and lightning zigzagged across the sky.

"Maybe we'd better head for that first motel," Emily suggested. "What was it? The Sea Cove?"

Jim shook his head. "No food there. I'm for going on to the Cliff place. Everybody keep an eye out for the sign."

A mile past the first motel sign, Jim glanced up from the odometer. "We can't be very far from it now. The guy at the gas station said . . ."

"Hey! There it is. Up on the left. See? There on the curve," Emily cried out. "There's the entrance."

Directly ahead were two high stone posts on either side of a broad drive. And as Jim swung into the entrance, they saw the name "Cliffspray" lettered down the length of one post.

"They sure don't believe in lighting up this sign," Jim said uneasily. "And wasn't the name Cliff*side*?"

Emily hesitated. "Maybe he said 'Cliff*spray.*' Anyhow, we've come about the right distance."

"I don't see any lights at all," Jenny said doubtfully. "But maybe there's been a power failure."

Chris groaned loudly. "Then here's hoping they

14

cook with gas. Man! I'm ready for about five hamburgers."

Jim started the wagon forward and almost right away the drive climbed steeply through a windy tunnel of wildly tossing branches.

As they rounded a second long curve, Emily called out, "Jim, let's turn around. I think it's a private estate. This driveway doesn't look motelish to me."

"Turn around!" Jim exploded. "Honestly, Emily — just where would you suggest?"

"I mean, turn around when you can. Naturally."

At that moment they emerged from the climb through the tree tunnel and the drive leveled off into a large open space. Beyond, they could hear the roar of crashing surf. "Go slow, Jim," Chris called. "I'd sure hate to miss this place and — "

"Keep going over the cliff," Jenny finished.

The twins' words of warning were not necessary. In a giant zigzag of lightning, Cliffspray loomed up straight ahead — a dark, towering heap of stone, shaped into dozens of turrets and cupolas.

There was a sudden hush inside the wagon.

"A haunted motel!" Jenny gasped.

A tremendous crash of thunder drowned out whatever anybody else might have said. Jenny came scrambling over the seat. "I'm riding with you, Emily," she quavered.

"And here all the time I thought you were the family storm lover," Emily laughed, putting her arm around Jenny's shoulders.

"Hey, look! Up there!" Chris exclaimed. "I saw a light just for a second. There it is again!"

"It must be a lamp," Emily said, peering ahead and upward. "I think it's on the third floor, and it's moving around. Jenny, you're probably right. There's been a power failure."

"We won't stay to find out," Jim said shortly. "Here's where we head straight for Alston — or even the good old Sea Cove."

"Where there are definitely no hamburgers," Chris sighed.

But as Jim swung around the circular front drive to head for the exit, the children saw how murderous lightning could be. A blinding bolt split down the length of a huge dead tree, standing by itself near the drive. There was a jarring crash, then an ear-splitting roll of thunder. The headlights shone on a broken mass of boughs and branches lying across the drive ahead.

Chris was first to speak. "Man! I felt that one right through my chest!"

There was a moment's pause before anybody said a word. Then Jim spoke. "I guess this is where we find out if we're at a motel or — "

"At a mad scientist's house," Chris added ghostily from the back.

Jim circled back along the drive and stopped

16

before the huge forbidding double doors of the dark mansion.

"Well," he said, "let's get this over with. As things look now, we may have to stop here."

He stepped out into the driving wind and rain, hurried to the doors, and pulled at the old-fashioned bell. In the station wagon, only the drumming sound of rain on the wagon roof broke the silence as the three inside watched a long, narrow slit of light appear in the doorway.

"It's opening," Chris breathed. "Somebody's standing there."

"Or some*thing*," Jenny whispered from the crook of Emily's elbow.

3

As the door opened wider, Jim took a backward step. In the eerie light thrown by the lamp she held, a woman's stony-hard, dead-white face thrust toward him. Below tightly pulled-back gray hair, pale eyes stared. The bony hand holding the lamp was streaked with raw red scratch marks.

"What do you want?" the woman asked in a hard, cold voice.

Jim gulped. "I'm sorry to bother you," he managed to say. "We thought this was a motel, and — "

She cut off his words. "It isn't. You can't stay here!"

The door began to close. Jim pressed hard against it.

"Wait, please, We *can't* leave. There's a tree down. It's blocked the drive. Could we speak with the owner, please?"

"*Owner!*" The woman's laugh was a harsh crackle. "You are speaking to the owner. I happen to be Miss Cliff, and I'll thank you to leave immediately."

"Miss Cliff," said Jim, pressing his foot against the door edge, "we *can't* leave. It's as I told you — a tree is blocking the drive. Is there another way out?"

"There is not. Now move your foot, young man, and *good night!*" Again the woman tried to press the door shut.

"Listen, Miss Cliff," Jim said desperately. "We're stuck here. And we're awfully hungry. Couldn't you fix us sandwiches or something, and let us just stretch out somewhere until this storm stops? We can pay you."

The pale eyes sharpened. "How much?"

Jim thought rapidly. This was no time to haggle over prices. "Whatever you say," he replied, still holding his foot against the door.

He turned and waved at the car, beckoning the family to come on. "Don't bother with any luggage now!" he shouted into the storm.

Chris, Emily, and Jenny hurried through the rain toward the half-open door, and followed Jim into the dark house.

The heavy door slammed behind them, and Miss Cliff, holding the lamp higher, stared at the rain-spattered group.

"We haven't told you our names," Jim began politely.

"No need to," she snapped. "You won't be staying long enough for me to bother about your names. Now — follow me."

She circled around them and moved quickly into the cavernous dark ahead. It was made even more sinister by the small circle of light cast by the lamp.

The light stopped abruptly, and with a bony hand the woman motioned them to walk to the left.

"I — I can't see," Emily said, stumbling forward.

"Oh — bother!" the woman exclaimed. She sailed on into what seemed to be a huge room, and went over to an immense fireplace. "There! Is that enough light for you, miss?" she asked, lifting the lamp up to the mantel.

"Oh, it's fine, thank you," Emily replied shakily, trying to peer into the shadow.

"Then sit down and don't wander around. I'll have no strangers snooping about this house."

With those rude words, Miss Cliff moved off toward the pitch dark of the hallway. An amazed group stared until the blackness swallowed her up.

"Well!" Emily exploded. "Jim, let's get out of here. Snooping around! Any time I'd snoop anywhere! And in a creepy place like this. I don't want to stay another minute."

"Well, I'd like to stay a minute anyhow," Chris said. "I'm hungry."

Before anyone else could say anything, they heard Miss Cliff's voice ring out of the dark beyond. "Alston!" she cried. "Alston!"

Jenny burst into giggles. "She sounds like a bus driver. Do you suppose she's calling out the next stop?"

"I heard that, young lady!" Miss Cliff suddenly loomed out of the dark. "It so happens my family founded the city of Alston. Who has a better right to the name than my brother?

"Alston!" Miss Cliff shouted out again. "Bring a spare lamp in here."

"Have you had a power failure?" Emily asked, trying to be sociable.

Miss Cliff's eyes stared coldly. "Power failure! Nothing and no one fails in *this* house. Remember that, miss."

Emily shrank back. Miss Cliff, after glaring for a moment, again disappeared into the hallway.

"I think she's *Mrs.* Cliff — wife of the mad scientist," Chris whispered to his twin.

"And her husband's going to be here any minute," Jenny whispered back. "I *feel* it."

Just then they heard a low heavy humming. It sounded dull and far away in the vastness of the room. Chris was the first to comment on it. "A generator!" he exclaimed. "That means they have electricity for emergencies."

"Then why use lamps?" Jenny asked. "You must be wrong, Chris. Maybe it's — it's a dam breaking and we're right in the path of a flood!"

"Don't be silly," Chris replied. "We're on top of a cliff. There'd be no dam up here. Listen!"

"I think you're right, Chris," Jim said as the humming steadily continued. "It's a generator working."

Goosebumps suddenly popped up along Chris's arms. "And I know why," he said in a low voice. "There *is* a mad scientist here. I'll bet he's down in the basement right now, juicing up some new kind of Frankenstein's monster."

Before anybody could say "don't be silly," Miss Cliff stalked into the room. "I don't like whisperers," she glared at the group. "Alston, come in here."

Behind her came the glow of a second lamp. And carrying it was a giant hulk of a man. Heavy wild-looking hair fell about his shoulders and a bushy black beard hung to his chest.

"Put the big lamp on the mantel, Alston. Then take the smaller one and go call Brother. Ask him what I should charge for bread and butter sandwiches."

"Bread and butter *sandwiches*!" Chris gasped. "We're starving, Miss Cliff. Couldn't we at least have bacon and eggs, or something like that?"

"We'd pay you well," Jim said hastily.

Miss Cliff hesitated. "Very well. Alston, go ask Brother if he thinks bacon and eggs are suitable, and how much to charge."

22

The giant shook his head. He pointed to the ceiling. "Brother — is — upstairs," he said haltingly.

Once again Miss Cliff seemed uncertain. Then she nodded. "We will wait then. Brother should be down soon. Go sit on the stairs, Alston."

The giant lumbered off and Miss Cliff waved her arm toward the huge pieces of furniture, covered with sheets like monster ghosts. "Sit down," she ordered, then left the room.

"Do you know what I think?" Jim spoke slowly. "I think that fellow at the gas station must have said 'Cliff-*side*.' "

Even Jenny, who had been staring fearfully toward the staircase, burst out laughing with the others.

"What's so funny?" Jim frowned.

"You," Jenny said. "That's what we've *all* been thinking ever since we got here." Her voice dropped low. "Cliffside — Cliffspray. It doesn't matter now. We're in a place we can't leave. We're *trapped*. I think this is my premonition I had this morning."

"Jenny, we're trapped by a fallen tree — not by a premonition," Jim said. "I wish you'd stop spreading gloom and doom all over."

"Jolly Jenny — that's your name," Chris giggled.

"Oh?" Jenny looked sternly at her twin. "How about grisly Chris? Who's been talking about

23

juiced-up monsters anyway? Not *me!*"

"Not *I*," Emily said almost absentmindedly. She turned to Jim. "Seriously, though — there might be a telephone around here. Shouldn't we ask?"

"Who'd we call?" her brother shrugged. "We shouldn't worry Dad and Mom. And anyway, what could we tell them about our plans? We're not going to drive out of here until that tree is cleared away, and no tree crew will start working on it tonight."

"Then what will we do?" asked Chris. "Sleep in the car?"

A new voice came from the dark-circled room. "You must spend the night with us, of course."

The group almost jumped out of the dust-sheeted chairs, as a tall thin man dressed in a lab coat stepped into the room. He walked toward them, holding out a bony hand.

"I am Dr. Cliff," he said. Pale eyes stared at Jim. "I just happened to be glancing out an upstairs window when I saw the tree struck by lightning. My brother and sister have explained how you mistook our home for a motel and are — er — *trapped* here." He smiled at Jenny, who flushed bright red. How long had the newcomer been listening to their conversation? And where had he come from so silently? Not from the staircase. The giant, Alston, was still sitting on the bottom step, lamp glowing beside him.

In spite of his welcoming handshake, none of the Blairs felt like smiling back.

There was something about him — it wasn't only the long red scratch mark down the left side of Dr. Cliff's face that repelled them, although that helped.

In the soft light of the lamp, they could see tiny droplets of blood had gathered into a small thin stream that ran from the sharp jawline onto the white collar below.

There was a moment's silence. Then Chris spoke. "You must have an awfully mean cat around here," he said. "That's some scratch!"

4

Dr. Cliff's hand flew to the side of his face, and he flushed. "Drat!" he exclaimed in an ugly voice, and drew from his pocket a bloodstained handkerchief.

"I guess it scratched your sister's hand, too," Jenny said. "Doesn't it like people?"

Dr. Cliff managed a smile. "You guessed right, young lady. If it weren't storming so hard, I'd put it right out the door. It acts like a wildcat."

There was another silence. This time it was broken by Miss Cliff's voice. "Brother, I have done your bidding. Bring those people to the dining room."

Dr. Cliff took the lamp from the mantel and led the way. Chris and Jenny trailed behind.

" 'Done his bidding'!" Jenny whispered, reaching for her twin's hand. "I bet he's a mad *hypnotist*."

Chris shook his head. "I still say he's a mad scientist," he whispered back. "I bet he's just designed a giant cat down there in the cellar and the cat can't stand him."

They hurried and caught up with the others at the dining-room door.

No matter what lay ahead, nobody was going to go to bed hungry at Cliffspray that night. Along a lamplit table were plates of hot rolls, sliced tomatoes, and a huge, partly sliced pink ham.

Emily halted as she stepped into the dining room. "My goodness!" she exclaimed, staring at the table. "And here I was, worrying about bread and butter sandwiches. I'm afraid we've put Miss Cliff to a lot of trouble, Doctor."

"But she'll make more money," Chris added. "This is going to cost a lot more than the original price, I bet."

"*Chris!*"

But Dr. Cliff smiled. "My sister is not a sociable person. But when she really understood your plight, she made every effort to make your stay here comfortable, as I knew she would."

"I guess it was your *bidding* her," Jenny said, blinking hard at their host.

For just a second a cold gleam shone from Dr. Cliff's eyes. Then he smiled. "Shall we be seated?" he asked.

It was when Miss Cliff came in with dishes of ice cream that Chris burst forth with a question about electricity that was puzzling him. "How come you can keep ice cream frozen when you don't have electricity here? Do you keep your refrigerator down in the basement?"

Dr. Cliff's eyebrows shot up. "Basement?" he asked, blankly.

"Where your generator's working," Chris nodded.

"Oh." Dr. Cliff frowned. "You heard it then." He leaned back in his chair. "I suppose this must seem a very strange old house to outsiders."

Every face turned toward him. No one spoke.

Dr. Cliff drew a knife slowly up and down the tablecloth. "Perhaps I should explain," he began. "You see, I am a scientist — "

"I knew you weren't an *M.D.* kind of doctor," Jenny said. "They hardly ever mind a little blood — like you did," she added.

Once again Dr. Cliff stared coldly at her. "As I was saying — I am a scientist. This old family mansion was closed many years ago. I have only recently fitted out a laboratory in the basement. I have had a generator installed for my needs, and as I expect to be leaving here shortly, it seemed foolish to have this old place wired throughout. My sister and brother, myself, and a visiting fellow-scientist, are quite comfortable with this limited arrangement." Again he smiled. "You see — we never expected to be mistaken for motel-keepers."

28

"Oh, we knew we'd made a mistake, but the tree — "

"Of course. The tree." Dr. Cliff sighed. "Well, we'll solve that problem tomorrow. Meantime, I believe we can make you comfortable here. My sister and brother are readying bedrooms upstairs now. You may find them a bit musty as they haven't been opened for years. But luckily we brought an ample supply of bedding with us."

"Does your fellow-scientist sleep up there?" Jenny asked quaveringly.

Dr. Cliff looked at her for a long moment before answering. "As a matter of fact, nobody sleeps up there — unless you count the Ghost of Cliffspray. Alas! I fear she doesn't sleep soundly."

"Ghost!" All four Blairs said the word together.

Dr. Cliff nodded solemnly. "At first I thought I wouldn't mention her to you. But then I realized you might hear her in the night and be frightened. There are other strange noises, too, which may be other hauntings. I suggest you simply stay in your rooms until morning, and you will be quite safe."

"You mean there is danger in the halls?" asked Emily anxiously.

"No, I don't think so. We have never confronted her, however."

"Wow," breathed Chris. "A real ghost!"

Jenny suddenly felt cold. She glanced at Jim,

but he was looking at Dr. Cliff. "You mean it?" he asked. "Can you tell us more about this ghost?"

Dr. Cliff's eyes gleamed. He leaned back in his chair. "Sure the story won't frighten anyone?" He glanced at Jenny, who blinked back at him steadily and shook her head.

Dr. Cliff laced his long bony fingers together. "Well, I don't know just when it began — but it was in my grandfather's time. Grandfather was also a scientist and quite famous. He built this great pile of granite rock and moved in with his family. No sooner were they settled than the Ghost of Cliffspray made herself known.

"Now everybody knows that there are ghosts in *old* houses, but at that time this mansion was newly built, so it amazed them when, for the first time, they heard the ghost cry out." He paused.

"Did she have anything to say, or did she just weep and wail?" Chris asked interestedly.

Dr. Cliff stared into the lamplight. "It varied. Sometimes it was a cry for help. Sometimes it was wailing. But the really frightening cry happened during storms. The ghost would wail, 'I am Andrea Cliff. This is my house. Please help.' "

Dr. Cliff sighed. "You can imagine my grand-parents' horror. There was no record of any Andrea Cliff in the family. And my grandfather *knew* whose house it was. His. He had built it. Of course, what might have been on this land before that . . ." Dr. Cliff paused, then continued. "But, as a scientist, my grandfather couldn't believe in ghosts."

"Do you?" Jenny asked.

"Certainly," came the reply. "But I believe science will solve the riddle one of these days."

"Is that the experiment you're working on now?" Chris asked.

"No." Dr. Cliff's reply was short. "Anyhow," he continued, "all those nightly disturbances finally drove my grandparents from this house. And for all I know, in all the years this old stone pile has stood here, that ghost has been calling out to nobody. We've certainly heard her wailing since we've been here."

His pale eyes gleamed as he leaned forward. "That is why we decided to sleep in the basement. She doesn't haunt us there!" He looked around the table at the staring faces, and Jenny thought he looked pleased at the effect of his words. "Now you will understand why I said, 'Stay in your rooms until morning.' "

There was a silence, then Jim laughed. "Maybe the way to solve the problem would be to go out in the hall and say, 'Hi, Andrea!' She sounds lonesome to me."

Dr. Cliff's sharp jaws tightened. "Do as you please," he said curtly. "I've warned you."

There was an uneasy pause. It was one thing to hear a ghost story. It was quite another thing to realize that the storyteller really believed in a wailing Andrea Cliff who stalked the dark old hall-ways overhead.

Emily shivered. "You won't find *me* saying, 'Hi, Andrea.' "

Dr. Cliff suddenly smiled. "Very sensible of you, my dear." He arose. "Now if you'll excuse me, I'll just go upstairs and see how my brother and sister are getting along with their task."

Before anyone could reply, he was swallowed up in the darkness beyond the table. They listened to the sound of his footsteps die away in the distance.

"Wow!" Chris exclaimed in a low voice. "IIe can see in the dark. Was I right or not? I kept saying he was a mad scientist."

"That's a very unkind thing to say, Chris," Emily said. "Dr. Cliff has made us welcome, and remember — he didn't *ask* us to come."

"And if it weren't for him, we'd have been dining on bread and butter sandwiches, remember." Jim grinned. "Personally, I think we've been very lucky, considering everything — and the fact that it's still pouring cats and dogs. Listen to that storm!"

Either the doctor's story had been so weird that everyone had forgotten the storm, or the wind and rain had increased. Drops splashed and drummed against the dark windowpanes at the side of the room.

"Man! We're going to get soaking wet, getting

our luggage out of the wagon," Jim said.

Dr. Cliff's voice sounded from the doorway. "No need of that, young man. My sister has provided for all your wants."

Jim jumped to his feet and the others pushed back their chairs, startled. How long had the doctor been standing there? Had he heard what Chris said? Jim's face flushed and he said hurriedly, "Thanks, sir. But I've left the keys in the wagon. I'd have to go out anyhow."

Dr. Cliff stepped into the light. "Foolish, my boy! Not likely your car would be stolen this night. Nobody can get in here. Remember? We're cut off from the world. Quite, *quite* cut off."

The man was stating a fact. But all the Blairs felt a slight chill at his words.

"I guess you're right, sir," Jim muttered, not wanting to sound unfriendly. But Chris suddenly remembered his own words to Jim only a few hours ago — "I hope you're not going to turn into an elder statesman." Now he wished Jim *would* take the lead and not let Dr. Cliff tell him what to do.

He *ought* to get the keys, he thought, shivering. Our wagon is all we've got that's *home*. But all Jim says is, "I guess you're right, sir." I think we're in trouble.

Dr. Cliff smiled his false host-y smile and beckoned them toward the hall. He was carrying a lamp, and the Blairs trailed after him into the

33

blackness. Each carried one of the unlighted candles that Dr. Cliff had distributed.

Jenny leaned toward her twin. "I don't care what anybody says," she whispered. "I'm not brushing my teeth tonight."

"Why not?" Chris whispered back. "He said they had everything for our 'wants.' "

"I know," she muttered. "But I for one don't want to trail down to any bathroom and meet a ghost on the way."

"I'd rather meet a ghost than one of the Cliffs," said her twin. "Ugh!"

"What'd you say, Chris?" Jim asked from in front of them.

"Just 'Oh,' " Chris answered. "Like in, 'Oh, here's the staircase, don't stumble.' Why?"

"Oh, just — keep moving," Jim answered. "I can't wait to get to bed myself. Man! I'm nearly dead."

Once again Chris shivered. He wished Jim had picked out almost any other word than "dead." He suddenly found himself thinking about Jenny's premonition of doom. Was it really hanging over them?

Then, as though Jenny had been reading his mind, she leaned close to him saying, "Remember what I said about a premonition this morning? *This is it.*"

5

Miss Cliff was waiting like a headmistress at the top of the stairs. She led the two girls along the hall to the room they would share. "The bathroom is through that door," she said in her rasping voice. "Luckily for you, my brother Alston was able to turn on the water for the upstairs bathrooms. You may leave the candle I've placed in there burning. But be sure," she ordered, "to blow out the candles in the bedroom before you go to sleep. This night is costing our family a great deal as it is, without your starting a fire."

Emily and Jenny hardly listened to Miss Cliff's lecture. They were staring fearfully around the huge room. Giant shadows crouched and leaped, yet the flickering candle flames were hardly more than pinpoints of light in the darkness.

Miss Cliff stalked to the hall door. "I advise you

to bolt your door. But then — do as you please. I, for one, would."

The door closed heavily behind her. For a moment the two girls continued to huddle together. Then Emily marched to the door. "Miss Cliff may be odd," she said, sliding the heavy bolt, "but I'm following her advice."

"Emily, are you afraid of the Ghost of Cliffspray, too?" Jenny quavered.

"No, and don't you be. But there's no point in taking chances. They're all queer, including Alston." Emily laughed nervously. "Give me a ghost any time," she said.

Jenny looked thoughtful. "Maybe we'll hear one tonight," she said darkly.

"Oh, Jenny! Forget the ghost. Do you want the single bed, or shall we share the double?"

"Let's share. I'd rather."

"All right, Jen, but don't twitch in your sleep. Now let's see what Miss Cliff left us in the pajama line."

Emily reached out to a stack of folded garments and shook out the top one.

Instantly, the two girls burst out laughing. Jenny rocked back and forth. "I think they're Alston's nightshirts," she gasped between giggles.

"Or striped flannel tents," Emily suggested.

There was a sudden rap at the door. Emily

whirled, clutching the nightshirt.

"It's Alston," Jenny whispered, "back for his nightshirts!"

"Hey, anybody there?" Jim's voice sounded faintly. Emily rushed to unbolt and open the door. Jim stood there, candle in one hand and a frilly bunch of long nightgowns over his arm.

"Any chance you girls need these?" he asked, holding out his arm.

Emily giggled. "Thanks, Jim, but you keep them. We've fallen in love with ours."

But even as she held up the flannel nightshirt, from somewhere in the darkness of the ceiling they heard a faint, long-drawn wail. "Please — please! I'm Andrea Cliff. Help me. Please!" The voice sounded hollow, muffled.

Jenny flung herself forward into Jim's arms. "The ghost!" she gasped. "It's the ghost."

All three stood frozen, staring up into the darkness. Then Jim gently pushed Jenny away. "*Ssh!*" he whispered, lifting the candle high and walking toward a dark corner of the room.

He pointed upward. "There's where the voice came from. See up there. There's a ventilator. Old houses have them."

Jenny peered up at a large square-shaped metal grill in the ceiling. "What's it for?" she whispered.

"For letting warm air rise to the floor above."

"It's open — a ghost could slip through it,"

Jenny whispered back. She suddenly sped to the door. "I'm getting Chris. He's there, all alone. Besides, he won't want to miss this."

In seconds she was back, with Chris close behind. "Has the ghost done it again?" she whispered when they were in the room.

Two heads shook, "No," and Emily held a finger to her lips.

But Chris moved directly under the ventilation grill. "Maybe it's because it thinks nobody's here." He looked upward. "Yoo-hoo," he called.

There was a second of silence, and then the hollow voice answered. "Ple-ase!" it wailed.

Chris bounced backward. "Gosh!" he breathed.

Jim frowned. "It must be Miss Cliff doing that — trying to make sure we stay in our rooms."

"Why?" Chris asked bluntly.

Jim shrugged. "Who knows? Maybe because she doesn't want people looking around. But one thing's sure — I don't believe in ghosts."

"Dr. Cliff believes in ghosts — at least he says so," Jenny said.

"And he's a scientist, too," Chris added.

"And why would it be Miss Cliff?" Emily asked. "That voice would be enough to drive anyone out of a room, and Miss Cliff almost told us to stay in."

"Maybe it's a record player. Maybe it's Alton's practical joke — or the doctor's."

Jenny shook her head. "It's a ghost. Look at

this room — this house. It was *made* for a ghost."
Emily glanced at Jenny's pale face and quickly
said, "But it's just a sad one, not scary."

Jenny edged closer to Chris. "I'd help her if I
could. Wouldn't you?"

"Sure," her twin replied. "But I guess we won't
have the time. We'll be leaving in the morning."

An odd look crossed Jenny's face. "I guess so,"
she said doubtfully.

Jim turned toward the door. "I'm turning in.
Sure you don't want these — whatever they are?
It's your last chance." He held one lacy gown under his chin. "Not my type," he grinned above the
frills of lace.

But nobody grinned back. "Maybe the ghost
wore them back in the days when she was real,"
Jenny said sadly.

Chris groaned. "Jenny, don't you remember?
This ghost came to a *new* house. It isn't likely that
she brought a suitcase full of nightgowns. Anyhow, she's stopped talking, so I'm going to bed."

"You know," said Jenny when she and Emily
were alone, "Dr. Cliff said the ghost talked most
during storms. I wonder — "

"Jenny, stop!" said Emily sternly. "Forget the
ghost and come to bed."

It wasn't until the occupants of both rooms
went to open the windows, before blowing out the
candles and going to sleep, that they discovered

the windows were covered by shutters — nailed tight.

"How're we going to get air?" Chris asked Jim.

"How'll we know it's morning?" Jenny asked Emily.

6

But in spite of closed windows and occasional thumps and wailings that could have been the wind, the Blairs slept soundly until Alston pounded a "good morning" at each door.

Jenny and Chris, each having dressed in the dark, were the first to emerge from their rooms. They met in the dim hall.

"I see the Ghost of Cliffspray didn't get you after all," Chris grinned.

"Certainly not," Jenny said, tossing her head. She was feeling much braver this morning. "Why would she? As Emily said, she was sad, not scary. All she wanted was sympathy."

"Mmm. Well, she lost her chance then, because we'll be miles away from the ghost by tonight." He fell into step beside his twin.

"Say," he asked suddenly, "were your windows nailed shut? Ours were all covered by shutters. Weird. I wonder what it looks like outside?"

"Ours were nailed, too," Jenny replied. She

eyed the hall doors on the right and left. "Maybe the windows in some of the other rooms aren't nailed shut. Remember? You saw a lamp upstairs last night."

"Let's look."

"I guess that would be what Miss Cliff calls 'roaming around,'" Jenny said. "But let's roam, anyway."

In a flash, Chris was turning the knob of a door to the right of them. Sunlight flooded a big room filled with old-fashioned furniture. "Wonder why they didn't let us have a room like this?" he said, walking to the window. "I think we must be on the ocean side — at the back of the house. Hey, Jenny! Look!"

Through salt-sprayed windows they saw the sea far below surge and foam over giant rocks.

"This is why it's called 'Cliffspray,' I guess," Jenny said. "I'd sure hate to fall down there. Come on. There's nothing but ocean as far as you can look."

"I see two ships," Chris said. "But okay. Let's try a room on the other side."

The two carefully closed the door behind them and crossed the hallway. The door creaked as Chris turned the knob and stepped into the room. "I guess this one must be near the place where we drove up last night," he said.

"We don't have to guess," Jenny said impatiently. "We can look." She hurried over to the tall windows. "There's the tree that fell! Isn't it tremendous? I'll bet it will take hours to get it out of the drive."

Chris went to the other window. "Not with Alston the Mighty on the job. There he goes. Man! Look at that axe he's carrying. It looks like a hatchet in his hands."

Jenny looked and shook her head. "I wouldn't say even Alston could get that tree chopped up. It's *big*. I think it's going to take electric saws and stuff like that."

Chris pressed his nose against the glass and tried to see the front entrance. "Hey, Jenny," he said slowly. "The tree's there, all right, and there's the driveway, and I can just see the corner of the front steps."

Jenny peered from her window, then moved over beside Chris. "So can I," she said. "What about it?"

Chris straightened up slowly. "What else should we see?"

Jenny looked at him. "What'd you mean?" she asked.

"Look again," Chris said.

"*Oh!* Our wagon!" Jenny gasped.

Almost at the same moment the twins whirled around and raced for the door, and just in time to meet Jim coming into the hall.

"Jim!" they gasped together. "Our wagon! It's *gone*."

"What a way for a day to begin." Emily groaned a few minutes later as she and Jenny hurried down the stairs after the boys. "Dressing in the dark, and now — our wagon gone."

"I imagine they drove it into a garage," Jim said soothingly. "After all, it didn't drive off by itself; even if it could, there's no way out of here."

"That's right," Emily said, her face brightening.

"Good morning! Good morning!" Dr. Cliff, dressed in a white laboratory coat, called from the foot of the staircase. "Sleep well?"

"Good morning, sir," Jim said briefly. "I *hope* it will be, anyhow. But right now I'm wondering. Where is our station wagon?"

Dr. Cliff's smile vanished. Whether or not he already knew of the disappearance, he managed to look as surprised as Jenny had been. He rushed to the big double doors. The Blairs rushed after him.

There was absolute silence until Emily spoke. "You didn't put it in your garage?" she asked.

As Dr. Cliff turned around his face seemed to show anger, dismay, and deep worry all combined, but he eyed the group coldly. Then: "What jinxes you turned out to be!" he exclaimed suddenly.

Jim took a step forward. "What do you mean by that remark, sir? How have *we* jinxed *you*? You said there was no way out of here. Believe me, we wish we had found that way last night.

44

We'd like nothing better than to settle our bill and drive out of here. But how can we do that if you've taken our car?"

Dr. Cliff looked down and slowly shook his head. He was silent for a moment, and when he spoke, his voice was low, almost gentle. "You shall have the explanation, and I regret speaking as I did." He drew his hand across his forehead and looked up. "You see, it's my poor brother, Alston. I should have guessed this could happen. But I'm sure your car is safe. I — I'm just angry with myself. I should never have allowed the keys to be left in it. But it was raining so hard. I never thought Alston would . . ." His voice trailed off.

"What about Alston?" Jim asked, frowning. "I'm sorry, but I don't follow what you're saying."

Dr. Cliff sighed. "Of course you don't. But please let me handle this, my boy. Alston probably has your car keys in his pocket. You see — well, I'm sure you've noticed Alston is a rather unusual person. Poor fellow. He's mad about cars. I made the mistake years ago of allowing him to take the wheel whenever we were on some lonely country road. Ever since, I've regretted it. And I should have remembered, last night, what a temptation your car would be to him."

Dr. Cliff steered Jim and the others back into the house. "We'll have you on your way as soon as the tree is cleared away. The car is not far from here, you may be sure. Meantime, have a good breakfast, and I'll go out to speak to Alston."

Jenny and Chris, last to go inside, exchanged glances. "I told you he was a mad hypnotist," Jenny whispered. "Look how he's steering Jim around — and right after he called us jinxes, too." She squeezed Chris's elbow. "If our wagon isn't right at the front door by the time we've had breakfast," she said, "I think we should — should *walk*."

"Where?"

"Home."

Chris sighed and shook off Jenny's hand. "Listen — maybe your 'premonition of doom' was the stolen car, but let's not look for more trouble. We're miles from even that town of Alston. So forget about running away. You sound like a little kid."

Jenny looked hurt. She drew back. "Okay. But when you're doomed, *just don't say I didn't warn you.*"

7

Miss Cliff served juice, eggs, toast, and milk in her grim way. Then, not even inquiring if the Blairs had slept well, she disappeared into the kitchen. The Blairs were just as glad. Jenny's thoughts may have been gloomy, but Miss Cliff was gloom itself.

Before breakfast was over, however, Dr. Cliff came back looking quite cheerful. He pulled up a chair and sat down.

"I'm afraid I sadly misjudged my brother," he began. "Alston said he wanted to get your car out of the downpour last night. So it's sure to be in our old carriage house. I told you — Alston loves a car. Poor fellow didn't want to see yours standing out in the rain."

Jim heaved a sigh of relief. "Did he give you the keys, sir?"

A faintly uneasy look passed over Dr. Cliff's face. "Now, you know, I didn't think to even ask. But he probably left them in the car. Anyhow, he's out there working hard on the tree."

Jim put down his juice glass. "If you happen to have a two-man saw, I could give him a hand."

Dr. Cliff nodded. "We can take a look around for one in the carriage house and check on the car keys at the same time." He glanced at his watch. "As soon as you're ready. I'm afraid my colleague is wondering if I'm leaving the work on our experiment entirely up to him. I should join him as soon as possible."

"Is your colleague the same as the fellow-scientist you spoke about last night?" Chris asked.

"He is."

"What are you experimenting on?"

"Plants," Dr. Cliff replied shortly.

"Plants!" Chris and Jenny exclaimed together.

"I'm a marine biologist. This area is a perfect spot for finding sea flora. Why, don't you approve?"

The twins looked quickly down at their plates. Chris flushed. "We just thought that with a fellow-scientist and a special laboratory in your basement, it would be something — well, plants sound like an awfully *calm* kind of experiment."

Dr. Cliff laughed strangely, and his pale eyes glinted. "Calm. That reminds me. Did you have a *calm* night, or did the Ghost of Cliffspray bother you?"

"Ghost?" Jenny asked blankly, then remembered. "Oh goodness! That poor ghost! She was *so* sad."

Dr. Cliff's eyebrows shot up. "You mean you did hear her?"

Jenny looked puzzled. "I thought you said definitely that we *would*. If we weren't leaving right away, I'd almost like to talk with her and find out why she haunts this house. All we did last night was listen to her."

"What did she say?" Dr. Cliff asked sharply.

"Just 'please,' and maybe 'help me.' But her voice was awfully weak sounding."

Dr. Cliff looked relieved. "Maybe the famous Ghost of Cliffspray is fading at last. I certainly hope so. It would be a help in selling this old place if word got around that the ghost was gone."

"I'd rather buy an old place with a ghost than an old place without one," Jenny said. "A ghost makes a place a lot more interesting, I think."

"Jenny," Jim broke in. "Dr. Cliff is a scientist. I expect he doesn't *really* believe in ghosts. Do you, sir?" he asked, smiling at the doctor.

Instead of answering, Dr. Cliff glanced at his watch. "I'm afraid this interesting conversation must end, for me at least. Time flies. Shall we go out and look for the saw?"

"And the keys," added Chris.

The big square stone carriage house, to which the curving drive swung down, was not far from the edge of the cliff. It would be tricky, managing that turn in the dark, Jim thought, as they walked toward it. Beyond, the Atlantic Ocean was a blinding sparkle of morning sunlight.

Dr. Cliff strode rapidly over the weedy drive. The Blairs followed close behind.

He walked up to the huge barnlike doors and reached for the heavy crossbar that held the doors shut. "Now if you'll give me a hand, boys, we'll take a look inside."

"Oh!" Chris gasped as the doors swung out. "It's big enough for a parking lot!"

It certainly was huge — so big that it made the cars parked there look small, even though one was a long black limousine, and the other a good-sized gray panel truck.

But only Jenny rushed forward. The others stood in shocked silence.

"Where's our wagon?" Jim asked bleakly.

Dr. Cliff acted as though stunned. He stared ahead, bony hands clenched into fists. "That *fool!*" he gasped. "*Now* what can I do?"

"What will *we* do?" Chris asked. "Where else could it be?"

Without answering, Dr. Cliff swung around and started, almost at a run, for the cliff edge.

"Oh, no!" cried Jim, following him.

The cliff dropped steeply down to huge boulders piled up by the sea. About thirty feet below them, pitched forward but held by giant boulders, was

50

the Blair station wagon. The back wheels were up in the air. It looked as though a light push could send it somersaulting to the crashing waves below. Everyone stood motionless, staring down in horror.

Then Dr. Cliff seemed to very nearly explode with rage. If he was acting, he convinced the Blairs. He shook clenched fists at the sky. "Why did this have to happen?" he shouted. "Now, of all times?"

He swung around savagely to Jim. "Everything was going well until you arrived. Oh, why couldn't you have kept on the road to Alston? Get back to the house — all of you."

Nobody budged. Jim's jaw tightened. "Don't talk that way to us, sir! *We* certainly regret our stay here — a lot more than you do. But right now I'd like to know what you intend to do about this!" Jim pointed to the car. "I want a garage wrecker in here *fast*. And I want a regular tree crew in here *fast*. As for going out to Alston, the sooner the better. I'm about sick of the idiotic situations around here — and — and — I demand *action!*"

Dr. Cliff stared at the four pairs of eyes flashing back at him. And another of his lightning changes spread over his face. He smiled thinly.

"Of course you want action — and you shall have it. I, myself, will call a garage. Indeed, I shall call your father. Where can I reach him?

51

There'll be no question about expense. I shall take care of that. Now — please, let us return to the house."

Without waiting for replies, he strode ahead, and the stunned group tagged along.

Once back in the mansion, Dr. Cliff steered them into the big room where they had sat the night before. "I know it's ridiculous," he said to Jim. "But I can't remember — did you tell me your last name, or have I just forgotten it?"

Impatiently, Jim explained who he was and why they had started on the trip home without their parents. "So you see," he said, "my dad already has enough worries on his mind. I'd like to speak to him myself. He was expecting a call from us this morning and he's probably already worried about not getting it."

"He'll probably start checking with the police if he doesn't hear from us soon," Chris added.

Dr. Cliff looked alarmed, then smiled a false, bright smile. "You say that your father is a doctor?"

Chris nodded his head smugly. "Yeah, and we have an uncle who is a criminal lawyer, and if we need any advice, he'll give it to us."

Dr. Cliff's eyes flashed. "I trust it won't come to that. Alston is hardly a criminal. He started out last night to do a helpful thing. And I can imagine what happened. He simply lost control of that big station wagon and when he saw the cliff ahead, he did the natural thing — jumped out the door."

"Natural!" Jim exclaimed. "It would have been *natural* to steer in some other direction, wouldn't it? Anyhow, Dr. Cliff, as you still seem to have transportation, will you drive us to Alston? I mean, after the driveway is cleared?"

Emily nodded. "Yes. We don't want to be in your way — and that's about the nicest thing I could say about what I'm thinking."

Dr. Cliff glared silently at them, then said mildly. "Come to the kitchen with me, Jim. The phone is there. We'll call your father."

Jim Blair had never been more disgusted in his life. He slammed down the phone. "Your line's dead," he said shortly. "Now what?"

"Ah! The storm, no doubt. Lines are still down," Dr. Cliff replied. "Young man, this is a terrible interruption of my day. Will you please join the others? I shall return presently. Right now, I must think."

Jim stalked out of the big old-fashioned kitchen, his thoughts swirling. *He's* interrupted! he thought to himself. If I were Chris, I'd say we *have* stumbled on a mad scientist. He's strange all right, and so are the others.

He had a sudden uneasy thought. "I wonder if that line *was* just knocked out by the storm, or if it's been dead for fifty years? That was an old-fashioned phone and it was gritty with dust. Well, I mustn't scare the kids with that idea," he muttered as he thumped along the hall.

All heads turned as Jim came into the room. "What's the latest?" Chris asked.

"Slight delay," Jim replied. "The telephone isn't working. So Dr. Cliff says, 'Let me think.'" Jim flung himself down in a big chair and a cloud of dust rose around him. "What a dump!" he said in disgust.

Jenny got up from the couch where she'd been sitting with Emily and walked over to Jim. "You know my premonition of doom?" she whispered.

"Don't start that, please, Jenny," Jim scowled.

But Jenny was not to be stopped. "It's *real*, Jim. Listen, *please*. I think we should leave right now. We could just run out of here, and go to Alston."

Jim nodded. "We'll leave, don't worry. But let's just hear what that man has to discuss, first."

Jenny pulled at his arm. "Please, Jim — listen. You see, when Tommy got sick I knew *that* wasn't my premonition because I kept on having it. It got worse when we came to this house. But even when we heard the ghost last night, I knew *that* wasn't it, either. It's that Dr. Cliff. I — I think he has evil powers. Please, Jim. Let's run."

Jim reached out and pulled Jenny down to the arm of the chair. "Jenny, honey, calm down and stop worrying. We'll hear what Dr. Cliff has to say, then we'll go — if that's the only way out."

Jenny stood up. "At least this time I hope *we'll* do the deciding," she said icily, "and not Dr. Cliff." She walked toward the hall. "I guess I'll go upstairs and look out windows. Nothing else to do around here."

"Aren't we going to help clear away the tree?" Chris asked.

"What for?" Jim sighed. "We'd have nothing to drive even if the driveway was as bare as a bone. Let Alston do something useful for a change. He got us into this mess."

"Then I'm going with Jenny," Chris stood up.

"What were you mumbling about to Jim?" Chris asked as he and Jenny climbed the stairs.

"About what I said to you — running away."

"Why not just walk? Even if Dr. Cliff is a mad scientist — and I think he is — what could he do against four of us?"

"Don't forget his fellow scientist," Jenny replied. "Together, they could probably think up something. Furthermore, I don't think they're experimenting with plants."

"Why not?"

"Why pick a dark old basement if you're going to work on vegetables and stuff? Plants need light."

Chris frowned. "I suppose they *could* be developing a new kind of mushroom. I've heard that mushrooms grow in damp dark places."

"And bean sprouts," Jenny added thoughtfully.

"Maybe they're inventing a new kind of Chinese frozen dinner," Chris suggested.

Jenny didn't even smile. "Could be man-eating plants," she said. "That would be more like him. Or perhaps — the Ghost of Cliffspray may be mixed up in this. They may be making ghosts."

"*Ghosts!*"

"Why not?" Jenny asked calmly. "They could produce all kinds of ghost effects. And I bet they'd make a lot of money. Ghosts are very popular right now."

"For — Jenny! You're the one who's mad. If you're going to invent a ghost, you wouldn't design one that went around saying 'please.' You'd have one that shrieked a lot. Besides, I agree with Jim. He said he thought it was a record player and Dr. Cliff was just using it to keep us from wandering around."

"There's only one way to prove *that*'s right," Jenny replied. "Wander around and find out why we shouldn't wander around."

Chris grinned. "Why not? Let's begin!"

"What we need to do is find the door to the stairs going up to the third floor," Jenny said. She looked up and down the hall. "And there are an awful lot of doors."

"Okay. Why don't you take one side of the hall and me the other?"

"It's 'I the other,' " Jenny corrected.

"Jenny — which are you going to be? A ghost researcher, or — or — Granny-*Pain* Blair?"

Jenny didn't answer that. She walked on ahead of Chris, saying, "The trouble with you is that you're not getting started on this project. Come on."

There were ten doors on either side of the hall, and, as the twins discovered, nine of them led to bedrooms, or bathrooms, or broom closets.

"This last one has to be the stairs," Chris said, reaching for the doorknob.

Before he could turn it, the door was flung open.

Out stepped Miss Cliff.

8

"What do you think you're doing here?" Miss Cliff rasped.

Jenny thought fast. "Actually, we wanted to get ready for lunch — brush our hair and see if we looked okay. But with those shutters closed in our rooms we couldn't see ourselves in the mirrors. So we thought we'd look for a room that isn't closed up."

Before Miss Cliff could reply, Chris spoke. "Do you happen to have a match for candles, Miss Cliff? That would be a big help."

"Botheration!" But she reached into her apron pocket and brought out several kitchen matches.

"If you hadn't put us in a room with nailed-up shutters we wouldn't be such a botheration, I guess," Jenny replied, holding out her hand for the matches.

Miss Cliff scowled. "I shall light the candles myself, and shall wait for you to brush your hair." She looked at Chris. *"Your* hair certainly needs brushing," she snapped. "Scissors would help even more."

Turning, she marched down the hall to their rooms. "I don't have all day, young lady. So don't dawdle."

Jenny followed her into the dark bedroom, and as she did, Chris flashed across the hall to his room and dropped to the floor on the far side of the bed.

Jenny's candle lighted, Miss Cliff went to the door across the hall. "Where are you, young man?" Jenny heard her call out.

Jenny lost no time in brushing her hair. She, too, was wondering where Chris had disappeared to. Quickly she stepped from the bedroom, closing the door behind her. Miss Cliff stood in the hallway.

"I guess he probably went downstairs, Miss Cliff," she said. "He doesn't like people to mention scissors to him. I expect he didn't even bother to brush."

Miss Cliff made a gesture to Jenny to precede her down the hall.

"Oh!" Jenny suddenly halted, partway to the staircase. "The candle! I didn't blow it out. Just a minute."

She raced back to her room. Just as she leaned forward to puff out the small flame, there was a quick rattling sound somewhere over her head, followed by a tiny thud as something struck the carpeted bedroom floor.

Jenny froze. Almost afraid to look, she lifted the candlestick and glanced around the ancient, faded carpeting. A gleam of gold caught her eye. Hesitating, she bent over. A *watch!* A little, gold watch — and it was lying directly below the ventilator grill.

Swiftly Jenny scooped it up and shoved it in her pocket. She couldn't risk calling out, but she waved the lighted candle slowly back and forth under the ventilator. "It will be a signal," she said to herself. Then, blowing out the flame, she raced back to the top of the stairs where Miss Cliff impatiently waited.

Chris, peering carefully through the narrow opening of his bedroom door, watched Jenny as she sped toward Miss Cliff. He waited until they had started down the stairs. Then quickly and quietly he went back to the last door down the hallway.

To his surprise, he found it still unlocked. Before him stretched a steep flight of stairs. Up he went.

Unlike the second floor, there were not many doors along the hallway, and Chris had to guess which one of them would lead to the room over Jenny's. He tried two. Each swung open easily, and each was bare of furniture. He went on to the third door. "This has to be the one," he muttered, and almost fearfully he tried the door.

60

It was locked. Somehow Chris had known it would be.

He stood there listening. Not a sound came from inside. Probably this is the room where they keep the tape recorder, he thought. Maybe Miss Cliff was putting something scarier on the recorder in case we're here tonight. There sure is something around here they don't want anyone to know about."

Then, as he turned back to the stairs, another thought leaped in his head: Supposing Jenny is right, and they're putting finished experiments up here? He shivered. I guess I'm glad the door was locked.

Slowly, he started down the stairs, more thoughts tumbling around in his head. "There's one thing I don't understand, though," he muttered aloud. "Why is Jim just *sitting*? Why should he wait for Dr. Cliff to decide what to do? Why doesn't *he* decide? Why don't we just hike to Alston, like Jenny says? Or maybe there's a phone in the basement lab. We ought to find *some* way to reach Dad — or the police." He shook his head. "Gosh. Jim doesn't act as though he's in charge at all."

But as he hurried down the last steps to the main floor living room, he heard Jim's voice, and Jim sounded angry.

"If that's your idea of the best plan, it isn't mine,

Dr. Cliff. *Wait* for the telephone lines to be repaired. *Wait* for the drive to be cleared. *Wait* for a wrecking crew to haul up the wagon. *Wait!*"

Chris arrived at the doorway in time to see Emily stand up and face Dr. Cliff. "And believe me," she said, "our dad has probably already called every motel in Alston. Maybe by this time, he has the state police out looking for us. We're going to leave this *minute*."

Dr. Cliff raised his hand. "My dear, I could never forgive myself if anything were to happen to any one of you fine young people. Think of the danger in trudging along a lonely road that may be flooded or washed out. And how foolish! Now please listen to me. My plan is quite sensible.

"Alston is working on a ramplike structure from some old lumber he found in the barn. It will be rough, but when it's finished a car can be safely driven over the debris from the tree! I shall use the panel truck and search out the nearest working telephone if I have to drive all the way into Alston. At any rate, I shall call your parents, explain everything, and set any fears they have at rest. And I shall also call a garage. I take full financial responsibility and shall so tell your parents. Perhaps your station wagon will prove to be in driving condition. Or perhaps you will have to take a plane home from the Alston airport. But this is NOT the time to take unconsidered action."

Chris looked from Jim to Emily to Jenny. She was the only one who didn't seem to be listening. Instead, she was staring into her cupped hand and frowning. She looked up as Chris walked over to her, and quickly shoved a hand into her pocket.

"I'm going outdoors," she said loudly. "And I think Dr. Cliff is right. We ought to stay awhile."

For the first time, Dr. Cliff beamed. "Excellent, Jenny. Why don't you and your brother amuse yourself on the grounds while the others make a decision?"

There was a satisfied gleam in his pale eyes.

"Jenny," Chris said as they walked around the corner of the house, toward the cliff. "I don't get it. First you say RUN. Now you say STAY. And don't tell me it's your premonition!"

For answer, Jenny reached into her pocket. "Got something to show you," she said. "Let's sit down over by the cliff — and with our backs to that awful house."

"See! There you go! One minute you say it's awful, and the next — "

Jenny interrupted him. "If you'd just listen a second, maybe you'd understand."

Chris dropped down on the grass. "Go on. I'm listening."

Jenny took her time before opening her hand. First she explained about the noise overhead in the bedroom, then about the thud on the floor.

"Come on!" Chris exclaimed impatiently. "Speed it up. What was it?"

"This." Jenny held out her hand. The small gold watch with its gold bracelet gleamed in the morning sunlight. "Turn it over," she demanded.

"A.S.C.," Chris read aloud. "Who's A.S.C.?"

"The Ghost of Cliffspray, I imagine," Jenny replied. "Don't you remember? Her name was Andrea Somebody Cliff."

Chris slowly shook his head. "Ghosts don't wear wristwatches, so — " He hesitated.

"So the ghost *isn't* a ghost," Jenny said. "Is that what you were going to say?"

"Then that explains it!" Chris exclaimed excitedly. "That's why they keep the door locked!"

"What door?" Jenny asked, puzzled.

Quickly he told her of hiding in his room until the coast was clear, and then going up to the third floor. "But I didn't hear one sound from that room. I don't see how we're going to find out much. We'll probably be leaving this afternoon, anyway."

"Well, we already know quite a bit, don't we?" Jenny asked. "We know they're probably keeping someone a prisoner. And it's probably Andrea Cliff."

Chris frowned. "I don't know about that. Why keep somebody in your own family a prisoner?"

"I could imagine those Cliff people doing about anything," Jenny replied. "The only thing I'm

64

wondering about is if she's even — even queerer than they are. Remember those scratches on Miss Cliff's hands, and on Dr. Cliff's face? And we haven't seen a sign of a cat around here."

"You don't suppose they have a Cat Woman up there, do you?" Chris asked.

Jenny shivered. "I don't know. Something's awfully wrong. But the ghost had a very nice voice when she said 'please.' I mean, it wasn't snarly like you'd think a Cat Woman might talk."

"You can't tell much by one word," Chris said darkly.

"You can, too. It showed she was polite — and needed somebody. I think we should try to help, and we've got at least a few hours before we go — *if* we go."

"Maybe we'd better tell Jim," Chris said.

Jenny shook her head. "I don't think we should. He'd probably say, 'Dr. Cliff, I demand an explanation!' And you know what would happen then. We'd *never* find out anything."

"We might," Chris argued.

Jenny shivered again. "I don't know — but every time I even think about that Dr. Cliff" — she paused, and her voice dropped low — "my premonition of doom just comes up and grabs me."

Chris groaned loudly. "Listen. While you're thinking about your premonition, think of this: If they're holding somebody prisoner up there — I mean someone they shouldn't keep a prisoner —

wouldn't you think they'd want us to leave as soon as possible? Instead, Dr. Cliff is just about begging Jim to stay." He shook his head. "Jenny, I think you're on the wrong track."

Jenny dug her sneaker heels into the rough grass. "Not at all," she said loftily. "You've simply added a new *dimension* to the problem."

"I have?" Chris looked rather pleased. "I thought it was only another angle."

Jenny thoughtfully nibbled a stem of grass. "Same thing — I guess. And it really is something to think about."

Chris suddenly sat up very straight. He stared at his twin. "You know, what we need is *action*. And I have an idea."

"What?"

Without replying, Chris rolled over on his stomach and wriggled to the edge of the cliff. Jenny promptly did the same. They looked down at the station wagon, and then at each other.

"What idea?" Jenny repeated, suspiciously.

"The signal flare case in the glove compartment — I'm going to get it."

Jenny looked horrified. "You're not, either! It's too dangerous."

Chris gazed down thoughtfully. "I've got on my boat sneakers. They keep a pretty good grip."

Jenny clutched her twin's jersey. "It's too much of a chance. Let's go back."

Chris sighed. "You sure aren't planning ahead,

Jen. Suppose we did rescue the ghost. We'd need help to get her away, wouldn't we? We're sure not going to get it from Dr. Cliff, are we?"

"I guess not."

"Then okay. *If* we're still here tonight, and *if* we get the ghost, then — then — " Chris paused. "Well, if we had any trouble we could signal for help," he finished.

"Help from where?" Jenny asked. "You're supposed to be at sea when you use one of those things." But she slowly loosened her grip on his jersey.

"We're almost at sea, aren't we? Ships are going by all the time, aren't they?"

"All right," Jenny said slowly. "I see what you mean. But I'm going with you."

"What good would that do? Be sensible, Jenny. Maybe somebody might come out of the house. You could sort of head them off. Tell the truth. Say I've gone for a walk." He looked at his twin's worried face and grinned. "Maybe I'll even bring back your toothbrush. Who knows?"

And before Jenny could even think, Chris had wriggled around and swung his legs over the drop.

9

Jenny sat frozen, unable to believe her eyes as she saw the tips of her twin's fingers disappear from the cliff edge. "Oh, Chris!" she longed to cry out. "Come back! Don't you want to live to be a teenager?"

Instead she forced herself to be silent, to edge closer to the drop, and watch as Chris inched slowly down the steep wall that was cracked and broken here and there.

Small pebbles and sand rattled loose from his toeholds and skittered downward beneath his sneakers. After one long look in the direction of the wagon, Chris made up his mind not to look again. And when he looked upward, he knew he mustn't do *that* again. One way was blue ocean and flying white foam. The other, a high rocky wall against the blue September sky.

By the time his eye caught the flash of sun on the wagon's chromium bumper, directly to his right, Chris had almost decided the trip wasn't worth it. His fingers felt skinned. His knees, under his jeans, burned from skidding against the rough wall. Carefully, he edged along the slanted side of the wagon, and even more carefully, opened the front side door. It seemed as though the wagon might jiggle loose at a touch, and the door seemed to weigh a ton when he tried to pull it open.

But it *did* open, and Chris scrambled inside. He reached back to the packed luggage and fumbled around until his fingers closed on one corner of the metal case. Then, losing no time, he stepped from the wagon, letting the door swing shut.

There was only one thing left to do before starting the upward climb — stuff the case under the back of his jersey and tighten his belt securely below it.

Then, taking a deep breath, he started the perilous climb back to Jenny.

Jenny, eyes squeezed tight shut, heard the scuff of pebbles that told her her twin was scrambling upward. "Are you all right?" she managed to call out.

Chris didn't answer. He was too busy and breathless making his way slowly up toward the top of the cliff. Almost shaking in fear, he heaved himself to the topmost hold. "Hey, Jenny! Wake up! Stick out your hands. This edge may not hold."

Jenny opened her eyes only for a second. She held out her arms and felt Chris's fingers grip hard around her wrist.

"Pull, Jenny. *Pull!*" he cried out.

Jenny tried to lift her arms back. "I — I can't," she gasped. "You're too heavy."

"Don't be silly," she heard her brother say. "You're on your stomach, aren't you? Just wiggle back as hard as you can. Your arms will back up with you."

Jenny wiggled until her arms felt as though they were pulling right from the sockets. "One more wiggle," Chris urged. "Jenny! Back up."

With a super effort, Jenny moved back. And suddenly the pull on her wrist stopped. She opened her eyes in time to see Chris push up to safety beside her.

"Did you get it?" she asked faintly.

"Sure," Chris panted.

And just in time.

From around the corner of the old house Emily appeared, crying out, "Hey, kids. Lunch!"

The twins stood up, waved to Emily, and started back.

Chris wiggled the case around to the front of his jersey. "Now I'll rush in the door," he said, "and you'd better sort of rush all around me in case somebody notices my *peculiar* shape."

Jenny giggled. "You do look as though you've developed an instant bay window." Then her face changed. "Chris, you don't think it will light up suddenly do you? It would spoil everything."

"Including me," her twin replied.

"Oh, *Chris*! What if it exploded!"

Chris looked very noble. "I'd be a living distress signal. Come on."

Chris and Jenny managed to get into the old house without anyone noticing the funny bulge beneath Chris's jersey. They sped up the stairs to wash. Chris stumbled around in the dark, managed to hide the signal flare, wash his hands, and join a strangely excited Jenny in the hall. Then they both rushed down to the dining room.

Dr. Cliff eyed them coldly as they hurried to the table. "As I was saying, I didn't realize until Sister mentioned it that the room shutters were nailed shut. Alston will attend to them as soon as he has finished his outdoor task — which should be soon."

"Don't do it for us. We won't be here tonight," Emily said.

Dr. Cliff looked quickly down at his plate. "Oh, it's only in case your father prefers meeting you here," he said. "That would probably mean tomorrow. I shall leave immediately after lunch, and will find out what can be done, and what is the wise thing to do."

Chris put down his hamburger. "Dr. Cliff, doesn't your fellow-scientist ever take time off to eat?" he asked, suddenly changing the topic.

71

Dr. Cliff's lips narrowed. "He is a *dedicated* worker — as, I might add, I myself would like the chance to be. Usually we take all our meals together in the laboratory. Unfortunately, I've had to divide my time ever since your arrival. This is simply a lost day."

"We could say the same," Chris said.

Jenny looked up. "I don't think this is a lost day. My goodness, it isn't raining or anything."

"That's right, young lady," Dr. Cliff said. His eyes flashed coldly at Chris. "And now if you'll excuse me I'll be off on my errands. You'll be intrigued to know that I am picking up some dynamite. We are using it in one of our experiments. I mention it only to warn you to keep a safe distance from the truck.

"After lunch, Sister is going to show you how to work the player piano. It is quite an antique, and I think it might amuse you."

Chris and Jenny exchanged glances. It looked as though there might be some delay in exploring upstairs for the mysterious A.S.C.

Miss Cliff marched ahead, leading them into the big front room. She flung back a huge sheet, revealing the yellowed ivory keys of an old-fashioned piano.

"Now watch," she said in her sharp, raspy voice. "I don't intend to spend my day showing you how this works. It's nonsense, if you ask me."

True to her word, Miss Cliff hurried from the room when the loud, cheerful jangling of the player piano began. And while Emily searched for song titles among the dusty stacks of oblong boxes that contained the music rolls, Chris and Jenny took turns operating the piano — and whispering to each other.

"How're we going to get upstairs?" Chris asked. "I mean everyone will think it's funny if we leave."

Jenny floated her hands over the fast-moving piano keys, pretending she was really playing. "Don't worry. I've just realized that this would be the ideal time to tell Jim and Emily what I found. Miss Cliff will stay out of the way as long as she hears the piano, and we can all figure out what to do."

"But I thought you weren't going to tell Jim."

"Changed my mind," Jenny replied. "After all, Dad did say, 'Jim, you're in charge.' And how can he be in charge if he doesn't have the facts? Besides, I've figured out a way to get into that room, but we'll need Jim to help."

Chris glanced around toward the front window where Jim and Emily were talking in low voices. "I think they're figuring out some plan for leaving in case Dr. Cliff says 'stay.' "

"That's why we have to talk with them," Jenny replied. "We can't just leave the ghost here forever, maybe, can we? We *have* to try to help."

At the window, Emily and Jim watched the

gray panel truck bump slowly over the ramp Alston had made, then slowly disappear down the steep, tree-lined drive.

"Jim," Emily was saying, "I don't like this. Why didn't Dr. Cliff ask us to go with him? He *knew* you'd want to talk with Dad, yourself. In fact, why didn't you just *say* you were going along, too? There's something gruesome about that guy, and I don't like the way things are going around here."

Jim nodded. "Neither do I. That's why I thought I wouldn't ask to go along."

Emily's eyes widened. "You mean you're *scared* of him?"

"In a way," Jim replied calmly. "He's pretty odd acting. In fact, the entire Cliff outfit is — well, gruesome. When we leave, we're leaving together. I don't think the Cliffs are too reliable — if you get what I mean."

Emily shrugged. "Maybe you're right about leaving together and I sure hope it's today. I'm all for walking out now."

Jim was going to answer, but he stopped when he saw Chris hurrying toward them.

"Just don't scare the kids, Emily," he muttered. He grinned down at Chris. "Say, I never knew you and Jenny were such musicians."

Chris grinned back. "And there's something else you never knew. Come on over to the piano. We want a private conference. We'll keep the piano going so Miss Cliff won't come busting in."

So with the piano pouring out fast noisy floods of music, Jenny managed to tell her story. The little watch was passed around and carefully examined while Chris changed the piano roll to another stirring selection.

"So you see," said Jenny, "A.S.C. is probably Andrea Somebody Cliff. And probably she's the Ghost of Cliffspray."

"Ghosts don't wear watches," Jim said sharply.

"That's what Chris said," Jenny replied. "And I think we agree. That's why we'd better rescue her, hadn't we?"

"Rescue her! This is the last straw!" Jim exclaimed. "And I'm going to demand an explanation from Dr. Cliff."

Chris and Jenny exchanged swift glances, and Jenny's jaw set stubbornly. "I was afraid you'd say that," she blazed. "You haven't paid the least bit of attention to my premonition of doom. In fact, you've *laughed* at it. But I'm feeling doomier every minute. And if you say *one* word to him, I — I just know what will happen. Nobody will leave here — ever."

Jim sighed. "Jenny, you're a real ray of sunshine in this dump. Why can't you ever look at things in some kind of reasonable way?"

Jenny flushed. "I'm the most reasonable person in this room. And I only wish somebody would pay attention. I have it all figured out. First, Dr.

Cliff only pretended he wanted us to go. He put Alston to work and everything, to make it seem as though we could. Then we find our wagon has gone over the cliff, and all of a sudden he thinks of a million reasons for our staying. He could have taken *all* of us with him in that great big truck if he weren't up to something funny. I'll bet he doesn't *want* anybody to come here to drag up our wagon. And why do you suppose he told us that story about the dynamite? It was a threat. I think he's going to dynamite our wagon right down into the ocean — and maybe with us in it!"

She looked around the staring group. "And if *that* happens," she said, "well — there'll be four more Ghosts of Cliffspray."

Emily was the first to speak. "Jim, did you say something about not scaring the kids? They're scaring *me* to death!"

"They're not scaring *me*," Jim said firmly. "Jenny, be logical. Do you think the Cliffs will just sit around and let us rescue this A.S.C.? When we leave here, we'll report it to the police and let them handle it."

Jenny's eyes flashed. "Okay. I *knew* I shouldn't have told you. You haven't listened to one word I've said, or we'd go upstairs this minute, get the ghost, and get out of here before Dr. Cliff gets back. If we don't, we're never going to have a chance to even *see* the police. I *know* it!"

Her words were almost lost in the stirring strains of "Stars and Stripes Forever." She was pedaling furiously and the dusty yellow keys moved as though an inspired ghost was playing them.

But Miss Cliff's voice was loud enough. She rushed in from the hall, shrieking at the top of her voice.

"Stop that infernal racket. Stop it this instant! I've had about all of this nonsense that I can stand!"

Chris froze. Then he quickly flipped the switch.

In the dead silence that followed, Jenny took a threatening step toward Miss Cliff. "Okay. It's off. But I don't think your brother is going to like this. He *wanted* us to play the piano."

Even Jenny was amazed at Miss Cliff's reaction. She grew pale, then flushed. "Brother would stop short of torture," she said in a strangled voice. "And that noise is torture." She looked almost pleadingly at Jenny. "But there's no need to mention it, is there?"

Jenny's eyes widened. "No. We won't mention it. We'll go up to our rooms and give you a rest if your brother Alston is through with the shutters."

Miss Cliff whirled to the staircase. "Alston!" she shrieked. "Get down here this instant."

In a matter of seconds, Alston came thumping

down the stairs, and obediently followed his sister toward the back of the house.

"Man! Did you see that!" Chris breathed. "Alston's scared of Miss Cliff, and Miss Cliff's scared of Dr. Cliff. Some family!"

Emily shuddered. "Jenny, Jim's right. Let the police find out what's going on here. For all we know, what's upstairs is worse than a ghost."

Jim nodded in agreement. "If it's a person named Cliff then she's probably a relative. And if the Cliffs locked up a relative, she must be something *really* terrible."

Jenny stood her ground. "Maybe they locked her up because she wouldn't go along with what they're doing. Anyhow, we could find out. There are four of us against one of her. And my goodness! She said 'please,' didn't she? And that's more than the Cliff family ever says. Let's go upstairs now and just try to find out something. Maybe she'd talk with us."

Jim glanced toward the window. He shrugged. "You can forget about it. Look who's coming."

They all turned to the window. The gray panel truck was bumping slowly up and over Alston's ramp.

Angry tears sprang into Jenny's eyes. "We've lost our chance — and just because we talked and talked. I wish I'd never told you!"

She started to rush from the room, and Jim

called after her. "Jenny, don't you want to hear what Dr. Cliff has to tell us?"

Jenny hardly slowed down. "Why? What for?" she cried back. "I know it already. *We're not leaving!*"

10

Dr. Cliff smiled broadly as he stepped in from the hall. "Well, well — the old player piano kept you busy, I see." He rubbed his bony hands together. "I suppose you are all anxious to hear the news?"

"We sure are," Jim said. "Did you talk with my father?"

Dr. Cliff nodded. "He was very understanding, I must say. And you'll be glad to know your young brother is getting along fine. As I suspected, your father prefers to come to Cliffspray himself, and will be here Thursday to meet you."

"*Thursday!*" three voices exclaimed.

Dr. Cliff's eyebrows raised. "That's what I said," he replied in a chilly voice. "Before calling your father I went to the local garage to arrange for a wrecker to rescue your car. Alas! The wrecker cannot get here until Thursday. So that is the earliest date that can be arranged."

"But I thought we were to fly home tomorrow

if we couldn't leave today," Jenny spoke from the doorway.

She marched straight up to Dr. Cliff. "I, for one, must be in school bright and early Tuesday morning. I'm a very dedicated student. And you know how it is when you're dedicated."

"I'm pretty dedicated, myself," Chris said. "I guess it just slipped Dad's mind that school comes ahead of everything. He's always saying that, isn't he, Jenny?"

"Always," Jenny nodded. "I suppose it must have been all that worry about Tommy, then hearing about the station wagon. The poor man has probably gone off his rocker."

"Jenny!" Emily exclaimed in a scandalized voice.

Jenny ignored her older sister. "Call Dad, Jim," she said calmly. "Set him straight on this. And that's my *final* word."

"It certainly is, young lady," Dr. Cliff replied. He turned to Jim. "I strongly suggest that you all consider your father's convenience and *mine*. I'll have no time and no gasoline to drive you in to call or take you to the Alston airport. In any case, arrangements are satisfactory to your father, so we'll say no more about it." He glanced at his watch. "Only two hours left before dinner-time. A day practically wasted."

"That's what I'd say, too," Jim snapped angrily. "I'd feel much better about this if you had let me go with you and speak to Dad myself."

"Ah! You doubt my word?" Dr. Cliff smiled unpleasantly. "Have no worries, my boy. Dr. Blair will be here on Thursday, you may be sure."

He turned on his heels and strode rapidly from the room.

"Well!" Emily's face was red with anger. "I don't know about the rest of you, but I'm walking out of here *now*."

"I think that's a great idea," said Jim. "I'll go tell our mighty doctor that he needn't worry about our taking up more of his precious work time. We can stay at the Cliffside Motel even if we can't leave until Thursday."

"I'm for that," said Chris.

Emily nodded. "You tell him, Jim."

"Not yet," Jenny said firmly.

"Not yet?" Jim looked surprised. "You're the one who's been practically hollering about leaving."

Jenny looked at him unblinking. "Yes, but not yet. Not until we get the ghost. I've *promised*."

Everybody stared. "What do you mean — promised? When did you do that?" Jim asked.

"Just before I came downstairs for lunch. The ghost thumped at me. And I asked her questions and she thumped back. First, though, I asked her why she didn't talk, and she didn't thump at all. So then I said, 'Do you have tape over your mouth?' and she went *thump thump, thump*,

thump. So I promised we'd get her out of there *tonight."*

Jenny turned to Emily. "So don't go telling Dr. Cliff we're leaving right away, because — because I *won't."*

Jim shook his head. "First things first, Jenny. Your ghost will just have to wait."

"Then I'll wait, too," Jenny said stubbornly.

Jim sighed. "I suppose you have it all figured out how we'll rescue her?"

"Through that grill thing in the ceiling," his younger sister answered promptly. "I'd get up there myself, but I'm not tall enough. But you and Chris could *easily* do it."

"You have a lot of faith in us," Jim said.

"Of course I have," Jenny replied. "That's why I promised."

Up in the girls' room, all eyes were on the ceiling grating.

"If that thing is screwed in place, we can't do anything about it," said Jim.

"Maybe it just pushes up," Jenny said hopefully.

"Think we could give it a try, Jim?" Chris asked.

"Sure, but we'll have to be acrobats," Jim replied. "I'll stand on a chair while you climb up on my shoulders. This ceiling must be fourteen feet high."

Chris rapidly figured. "Well, the chair's about two feet high, and you're six feet. And then there's nearly five feet of me. Plus lifting my arms. That would be plenty."

"Okay. Somebody lock the door, and we'll start."

The next few minutes were tense. The girls held the chair steady, and Jim crouched to his knees while Chris climbed up on his shoulders. Slowly, Jim stood up, as Chris swayed dangerously from his shoulder perch.

He raised his arms and pushed up hard on the grate. The rusty old metal jolted upward, and Chris slid it to one side. He grabbed the sides of the open square and hoisted himself up to his waist.

"Hey! You're kicking me!" Jim exclaimed, trying to duck Chris's sneakers.

"Grab my ankles, will you? Push!"

Jim grabbed and pushed while Jenny and Emily steadied the chair.

"Okay," Chris called down. "You can let go." With one more heave, he disappeared from sight. Then, about a second later, his face looked down at them from the opening. "Got a pocket knife?"

Jim handed his up. More silence. Then Chris's face appeared again. "They had her hands tied behind her back," he told them. "Her mouth is taped. I've untied her but she's afraid to rip off the tape."

"You do it," Jenny called up softly.

"Not me. You're the medical expert in the family. Now here she comes. Ready?"

It was a good thing that the Ghost of Cliffspray was athletic, or all of Jim's and Chris's efforts would have been in vain. Andrea S. Cliff might have become a real ghost. But she planted her navy blue sneakers firmly on Jim's shoulders, tugged Chris's dangling hands to signal "Let go," and with a neat swing of her denim-clad legs, did a midair flip-flop to the floor.

It took a second for anyone to react. "I guess we were expecting somebody more *ghostly*," Jenny said, staring at Andrea's long dark hair, her striped jersey, and her blue jeans.

She stepped forward, and with one swift jerk, peeled the tape from Andrea's mouth. "Now that didn't hurt much, did it?" she asked in a bedside manner.

Andrea Cliff rubbed her lips with a swollen hand. She tried to smile. "Hardly felt it. Thanks."

Chris's descent wasn't as graceful as the Ghost of Cliffspray's, but with everybody's help he was soon safe on the floor.

Andrea looked at them gratefully, one by one. "I'd just about given up hope," she said. "Thank you, *everybody*."

"At first we thought you were a ghost," Jenny said.

"Or a record player," Chris added.

Andrea looked puzzled. "I heard you saying things about a ghost, and about a record player, but why?"

Jenny pointed to the ceiling. "It was when you called from up there last night."

"*Called from up there!*" Andrea exclaimed. "I didn't call you from anywhere."

"But you did," Emily said. "Don't you remember? You told us your name and asked us for help."

Andrea shook her head. "I certainly wanted help. But I couldn't have called. My mouth was taped. My goodness! I couldn't have made a peep!"

"But we heard you," Jenny insisted. "You said, 'I'm Andrea Cliff. Please help me.' *Aren't* you Andrea Cliff?"

Andrea's face paled. "Yes," she replied, in almost a whisper. "But I didn't call. I couldn't have."

There was an uneasy exchange of glances. They had found the ghost of Cliffspray, and yet . . .

Then Emily spoke reassuringly. "Well, it must have been a pretty frightening experience. Maybe, in all that struggle with our charming hosts you just forgot — well — *when* you were 'taped.' "

"I've forgotten *nothing!*" Andrea's pale cheeks turned pink. "I was scared up there with the wind wailing and the floors creaking, but I'm not mixed up, if that's what you're all thinking."

"Never mind," Jim said hastily. "It was probably a record player that the girls heard. That's what I thought all along."

"Then why didn't Andrea hear it, too?" Jenny asked him. "The voice sounded as if it was right in her room. Maybe it wasn't really. Maybe it was piped, but . . ." Her voice trailed off.

Chris jumped up impatiently. "It looks to me as though somebody would ask something useful — like, 'When do we leave?' "

Andrea's face, which had been angry, now had a strange faraway look. "Do you believe in ghosts?" she asked slowly, as though she hadn't heard a word Chris had said.

"You mean the Ghost of Cliffspray?" Jenny asked.

"How did *you* know about her?"

"Dr. Cliff told us."

"Dr. Cliff! You mean you've *talked* with my father?"

It was Chris who restored order. "Listen, everybody," he said. "Why don't we let Andrea tell her story — all of it? And we won't interrupt." He turned to Andrea. "But make it short, will you? We want to get out of this place."

Andrea nodded. "Okay," she said.

11

"First," she began, "my father *is* Dr. Cliff, and he's a famous botanist. We came here — it must have been the day before you came — to see about selling this old place. You see, my great-grandfather built it years ago, but the house was haunted as soon as it was built — some say there was a woman lost over the cliff in a storm, long ago."

"Whew!" gasped Chris, thinking about his own recent descent over the cliff.

"Anyhow," Andrea went on, "my great-grand-parents left the house, saying that the ghost had driven them away. When Dad was a boy, his family did reopen Cliffspray for just one summer. But they all heard the ghost — in fact my grand-mother claimed it lured my father out of this bed-room, almost to the edge of the cliff one night. My grandparents were so frightened they also moved out and never came back.

"Then, about a month ago, Dad had an offer to

88

sell Cliffspray as a summer inn. With the reputation it had for being haunted, I guess there hadn't been too many offers to buy it. We came up here from our home in North Carolina to close the deal — as the real estate people say.

"But Dad wanted to look it over first. He showed me the whole place — right up to the attic. *Almost* all over it, I should have said. Because just before we were going to leave, he remembered an old lab in the basement he had rigged up that summer when he was a boy. So he asked me to get the flashlight from the car."

For the first time, Andrea's voice trembled. "Well — out I went. When I came back, Dad wasn't there. I walked out to that old kitchen. He wasn't there, either."

Tears sprang to her eyes and she blinked them back. "I — I opened the door I thought would lead to the basement steps. And — and I didn't need a flashlight. It was as bright as day. I went down the steps. As I passed the first door, I heard voices and bumping around." She swallowed hard. "I rushed in, and there were two men struggling with Dad. Before I could even move, a tall, skinny woman grabbed me. She yelled out, 'Alston!' And a giant man with a bushy black beard rushed up.

"They hauled me back up the stairs, then on up a second flight of stairs. And they locked me in a room." She paused. "I — I haven't seen Dad since."

"I guess that's the whole story, then?" Jim asked.

"Just about," Andrea replied. "Last night I was watching the storm from the window when that awful man who wears a lab jacket came in, carrying a lamp. He was just starting to walk up to me when there was a terrible flash of lightning. We both looked out the window, and that was when we saw car headlights coming up the drive. They circled up, then on around, and then came back. We both knew why — we saw the tree hit by the next lightning bolt and saw it come crashing down.

"Well, I guess you know the rest better than I do. All I can tell you is that the man in the lab jacket hurried away. Later they dragged me up there." She pointed to the ceiling.

"About all I could do was what I had been doing — kicking and scratching. But this time, that woman got the giant to tape my mouth and tie my hands behind my back."

"That must have been while we were eating," Emily murmured.

Andrea smiled faintly. "I wasn't so lucky. Anyway, I had a terrible time getting my watch loose. But I did, and they'd forgotten I could still *hear*, and *thump* — which I did."

"Didn't you see anything in that basement room to give you a clue about what was going on?" Jim asked.

Andrea shook her head. "I must have seen the whole place, but I can't remember anything but some kind of a wooden frame and everybody shoving Dad around."

"But probably they *thought* you saw everything," Chris said. "And that's why they put tape on your mouth so you couldn't yell for us and tell us what was going on."

Andrea shuddered. "It's something awful. I know that."

Jim jumped up. "We'd better all get out of here, *fast*, and get the police on this. Don't worry, Andrea. They'll rescue your dad, and they'll get the phony Cliffs, too."

Chris nodded. "What we need now is *speed*. I sure wish our station wagon wasn't halfway down the cliff."

"So that's why you're still here!" Andrea exclaimed. "What happened?"

"Tell you while we're hiking out of here," Jim said. "Everybody ready?"

"Wait a minute!" Andrea reached into the pocket of her jeans and pulled out car keys. "If anybody knows where Dad's car is, we won't have to hike. Here's my duplicate set."

"Wow!" Chris exclaimed. "But how are we going to get to the carriage house without anybody stopping us?" He looked at Jim. Then he said, "Say! I have an idea. Fake Cliff left the truck out front, didn't he? If he hasn't put it away yet, you could say you'd do it for him. You're about the only one, Jim, he might respect and trust."

"Great idea, Chris! I could back out Andrea's car, whizz up, you'd all hop in — and *zoom*. Out!"

"I'll go to our window and check on the truck," Chris said, hurrying to the door, unlocking it, and speeding across the hallway.

In seconds, he was back, a strange look on his face.

"What's the matter?" Emily asked quickly. "What's wrong?"

Chris spoke slowly. "The truck's there, all right, but so's Alston. And he's been piling wood on top of that ramp." He paused, then said, "I guess *we've* been prisoners, too, all along."

A look of alarm and dismay spread on every face but Jenny's. She sat, arms clasping her legs and chin resting on her knees.

Jim sighed. "It was a great idea while it lasted, but I guess we walk. And after all, they can't stop five of us."

Jenny lifted her head. "I guess they can," she said in a quiet, deadly voice.

"What do you mean?" Jim asked. "And if you say one more word about your premonition of doom, I'll — I'll leave you behind. Honestly, Jenny — I'm beginning to think you *attract* bad luck."

Jenny's chin trembled, but she spoke calmly. "I guess maybe you're right. It's all been my fault —

making such a fuss about leaving and getting the ghost first. I — I wish we'd never rescued you, Andrea."

"*Jenny!*"

Jenny leaped to her feet. "Well, I do wish we hadn't. Don't you see? Don't you *understand?* That talk about a wrecker coming Thursday was just *talk.* Whatever they're doing in the basement will be finished by Wednesday. And we'd just wake up Thursday morning and find nobody home. Why do you think they were keeping Andrea *just* a prisoner? They could have murdered her if they'd wanted to. And now when they find she's with us, they'll think we all know about the awful thing in the basement. Why, they may murder *all* of us!"

She flung herself across the bed and burst into sobs. Her sister flew to comfort her, but Jim caught at Emily's elbow. "Now just a minute," he said sternly. "Jenny, you'd better get hold of that imagination of yours. Nobody's going to murder anybody. We're walking out of here together. Now. Understand?"

Jenny raised a tear-stained face. "We are *not,*" she said. "What happens to Dr. Cliff — the real one — if we do that? Don't you see? He'd be their *hostage.*"

In the stunned silence that followed, there was a sharp rap at the door.

"Duck!" Jim whispered to Andrea. She scrambled under a bed as Jim called out, "Come in."

The fake Dr. Cliff entered. "Ah!" he smiled in his thin-lipped way. "All together and admiring the oceanside view. Yes? Lovely at this time of evening, isn't it?" He glanced at Jenny. "What have we here? Tears?"

Chris quickly plopped down beside his twin. "She's been crying about missing school. And I feel pretty bad about it myself."

"Oh? Thursday is not such a long way off, is it? Cheer up. Meantime, I came to tell you my sister will serve dinner in about fifteen minutes. Please be prompt."

This time, his smile was sharklike. He turned to the door, leaving it open behind him as he went back down the hall.

"Come on," Jim said loudly, hoping his voice would carry down the hall. "Let's give the girls a chance to get ready for dinner."

He walked out into the hall and watched Fake Cliff go down the staircase and out of sight. Then swiftly he turned back into the room. "Action stations!" he whispered, taking out his pocket knife.

He handed it to Emily. "You rip a sheet. Make strips about three inches wide. Chris, you begin winding them into balls. Better make two — one for the girls, the other for you and me. Andrea, you help, and give me your car keys, will you?"

"What are you going to do? Get Andrea's car?" Chris asked.

"Give the keys to Alston," Jim grinned.

"Alston!" Chris gasped. "Man! You'd better warn Andrea that she may be out of transportation back to North Carolina!"

Jim turned to Andrea. "Alston's pretty crazy about cars. But with that barricade in the drive, I figure he could drive in circles to his heart's content."

He turned to the others. "And while Alston's doing that, we're going to tie up Fake Cliff and his sweet sister. I'll take on Fake Cliff. Emily and Andrea will rush Miss Cliff.

"Now here's the plan. Chris, when *both* fake Cliffs are in the dining room, you pretend to choke on something. That'll be the signal. You rush out, and I say, 'Excuse me. I'd better help him.' Then, Andrea, you'll be waiting right there in the hall. You keep one ball of strips, hand me the other. We all rush back in. And I want plenty of hullabaloo — real confusion. Got it?"

With a look of excited astonishment, they all nodded.

"What's my job?" Jenny asked.

Jim laughed. "Begin repeating five hundred times, 'I don't have a premonition of doom. I don't have a premonition of doom.' "

At the hurt look that sprang into Jenny's face, Jim reached down and hugged her. "I was just kidding, Jenny."

But Jenny pushed him away. "You may tell

them I have a headache and will *not* appear at dinner," she said icily. "In fact," she added threateningly, "I may not get over it for *months*."

"Aw, come on, Jenny," Jim said coaxingly. "See! My advice is working already. You've just proved it. You're talking about months from now, aren't you? You're not going to be murdered after all."

Jenny's chin set stubbornly. "I shall *not* take part in that — that *hullabaloo* you're planning. I'm taking your advice and I'm going to work on a doomless future."

When Jenny's chin took that stubborn set, the Blair family knew she meant what she said.

"Okay," Jim said. He hesitated. "Still friends?"

Jenny's arms suddenly reached up around her big brother. "Forever and ever," she whispered.

Chris moved impatiently. "This is getting too mushy for me. I thought we were in a hurry."

Jim grinned and started for the door. "See you at dinner," he said. "All angles covered."

But Jim wasn't quite right. Only almost all angles. One was completely overlooked. And it was a terribly dangerous one to have forgotten.

12

If anyone had asked Jenny Blair why she wouldn't go with the others, there could have been only the answer she had been forbidden to mention — her premonition of doom.

It was building up higher and higher. Tighter and tighter.

Something's wrong, she thought miserably. There's *something* Jim didn't think of. I just *know* it. But *what*?

And suddenly that missing something hit her with such a jolt she felt breathless. She had remembered the third man — the man who had helped the fake Dr. Cliff grapple with the real Dr. Cliff while Alston and Miss Cliff dragged Andrea upstairs.

Fake Cliff's "colleague" was on the loose — and dangerous! "Oh! I have to stop Jim. Fast! I'll warn Andrea!"

In a flash, she was out of the room and heading down the hall — but only in time to see Andrea dash down the staircase as the signal of loud coughing sounded in the hall below.

Jenny almost flew down the steps. Too late! Jim was already striding out of the dining room and snatching up one ball of strips from Andrea. He rapidly turned back to the doorway, Andrea following with the other, and Chris close behind.

With all her strength, Jenny made a flying leap, calling out "Chris," as loudly as she dared — and landed smack on the stone floor, one hand holding tight to her twin's ankle.

Chris jerked around. "What — Jenny!" He pulled his leg forward as hard as he could.

Jenny hung on harder, and from inside the dining room came a piercing shriek, a shout, and the crash of overturning chairs.

No need to whisper now, and Chris didn't. "Let me loose. Let go!"

"Please, please. We've got to save them. We're the only ones who can do it!"

Chris hesitated, bent down, and jerked Jenny to her feet. "What are you talking about?" he demanded, grabbing her wrist and tugging her toward the dining room.

Jenny tugged back. "Not that way. Upstairs. Quick!"

The uproar in the dining room was now so loud that no one inside would have heard a word from the hall. At the top of his lungs, Fake Cliff was roaring out, "Alston! Alston! Monty! Monty! Help!"

Chris suddenly stopped pulling away from Jenny. "Who's Monty?" he asked blankly, dropping her wrist.

"Tell you later. Come on!" Jenny answered, heading for the stairs.

"Where'd you hide that flare thing?" she puffed as they raced up the steps.

"In my bed."

"Do you know how to work it?" Jenny asked, following Chris into the boys' bedroom.

"I think so," Chris replied. "Get a light going, will you? The matches are beside the candlestick." He dropped to his knees beside the bed and lifted one corner of the mattress. "Who's Monty?" he asked.

Jenny paid no attention. "Maybe there'll be instructions," she said, dropping down beside him and holding the candle high.

Chris sprung one end up on the metal box and the top released. "Man!" he breathed. "Look at that! It looks almost like a real pistol. Almost. It's too fat."

The metal box was divided into three sections — the broad-muzzled flare pistol in one, and in the second, long tube shapes marked "parachute flares." The third section held the same tube shapes marked "comet flares."

Jenny snatched up a single white sheet and read aloud:

" 'THIS IS NOT A WEAPON. IT IS AN EMERGENCY DISTRESS SIGNAL. TO KEEP IT IN GOOD CONDITION FOR USE AT ALL TIMES, USE . . .' "

Jenny's voice trailed off. "It doesn't say how to work it," she said in dismay. "The rest is all about oil and wire brushes."

"We don't need instructions," Chris said. "It isn't a real gun. Those things are cartridges. They just pop down the muzzle, then you point it right up in the air and pull the trigger. They do it all the time in danger-at-sea movies."

Jenny nodded. "I remember now. But those just *whisshh*. And we need noise. *Lots* of noise, so people will come from miles around. Chris, what can we *do*?"

"I don't even know what we're doing it for," Chris answered, half angrily.

"Because of Monty."

"Who's Monty?"

Jenny quickly explained. "So you see only two of them are being tied up in the dining room. Alston's on the loose and so is that Monty. He'll probably get Alston, and then he'll have the jump on all of us. And when Fake Cliff and his sister are untied, *then* what happens? We'll all be goners!"

100

Chris looked horrified. "Our gooses will be cooked."

"Geese," Jenny said. She suddenly jumped up. "Chris, Fake Cliff said he was getting dynamite. Remember?"

Chris nodded. "But he didn't bring it in the house. Maybe he left it in the truck." He ran to the window. "The truck's still there."

"We'll have to try to get that dynamite," Jenny said determinedly. "We *have* to have an explosion."

"Jenny, are you crazy? I don't know for sure how to shoot those flares, and I sure don't know anything about *dynamite*. What are you talking about?"

Jenny stared. "I know what we can do. Use kerosene."

"That won't make a noise."

Jenny made a rush for the door. "Blow the candle out," she called back, "and bring the sky ammunition."

She scooped up the few matches on the old marble-top chest. "I'll get that lamp on the mantel in the front room. It's full of kerosene. You try the front door. If it's locked, we'll have to smash a window."

Together they raced down the hall and on down the stairs.

Scarcely had they reached the bottom step than

the shouts and noises from the dining room came to a sudden stop. Chris and Jenny froze.

"Ssh!" Jenny held a finger to her lips. "Listen!"

A heavy, coarse voice reached their ears. "That's right. Just stop it right there, or the Ghost of Cliffspray goes straight to Ghostland. Get me?"

"Monty!" Jenny whispered. "Quick! Be quiet!"

By now, Chris's heart was pounding as hard as Jenny's. On tiptoe he hurried to the big front doors — and out. One lucky break, he thought.

Hardly had he reached the truck when Jenny came hurrying out, clutching the unlighted kerosene lamp in her hand.

"Are the doors open?" she panted.

Chris turned the handle and the door of the cab swung back. He climbed up. "Nothing here on the seat."

"Look in the back."

"Can't. It's closed off. Try the back doors," Chris said, hurrying down.

Jenny's heart sank. "They're locked — probably because the dynamite's there."

Just then, the long sweep of headlights came from the carriage house. "Duck! It's Alston!" Chris cried.

"At least he isn't in the dining room," Jenny breathed. She scurried under a lilac bush just as a long black car with North Carolina license plates swept sedately along the big circular drive. "I've got an idea," Jenny said. "But we'll have to be

102

careful. We don't want to get in Alston's way. He'd probably jump out of the car when he saw us, and let 'er roll."

"What's the idea?"

"The idea is to go down there by the barricade. We'll have to collect some of the wood chips and shavings. Then we'll pour the kerosene from the lamp on it."

Chris shook his head. "It won't make much of a fire for long."

"Long enough," Jenny replied. "Besides, we can feed it. There's enough wood there. Then we're going to flag down Alston and make him give us a push."

"Give us a push! But you just said to keep out of his way," said Chris in bewilderment.

"Not *us*, silly! Fake Cliff's truck. All it needs is a little start and it would roll straight into our fire. I think it would get pretty hot, don't you?"

"Hot! With grease all over the bottom and a tank of gas in it, and — "

"Dynamite," Jenny added calmly. "Now here's what we do. Every time Alston passes us, we run. And we duck every time he comes up on us again. We get down to the barricade and get our fire lighted, then we race back up to the circle and flag him down."

"We hope," Chris said.

"We hope," Jenny repeated solemnly.

It didn't take too long for Chris and Jenny to

make it to the barricade — Alston couldn't have circled more than five times. But it took longer to get a dry heap of chips, shavings, and some drier twigs together.

"We'd better light it wienie-roast style," Jenny said. She pulled a small handkerchief from her jeans, tied it to the end of a long straight stick, then sopped it in the base of the lamp.

Chris took the lamp and carefully poured the kerosene over the heap of shavings and chips at the barricade. Then he made a tiny heap of dry leaves a distance from the main heap and touched a match to it. "Okay, set."

He ran to her side, took the long stick, and lowered the kerosene-soaked handkerchief end into the flaming leaves. Then picking up the signal flare case in one hand, and holding the stick like a spear in the other, he calmly said, "Here goes. Get ready to run." He hurled the flaming stick forward.

With a roar and a blaze of light, flames hissed and leaped skyward. Chris and Jenny didn't stay to watch their success. They tore up the drive to reach the circle before Alston could pass them.

Jenny waved her arms wildly at the big car. "He's slowing down," she said excitedly.

Whether Alston wanted to enjoy the sight or pick them up wasn't important, but he rolled to a stop.

Jenny opened the door. "Say, Alston — want to do something for us?"

He smiled. "Ride?"

Jenny and Chris climbed in. "Just up to the truck, Alston," Chris said. "Stop right behind it, will you? We'll get out there. Then when we say 'go!' you give the truck a push. Okay?"

"But don't follow it," Jenny warned. "Okay?"

Alston beamed. "Okay." He nodded happily. "One bump. Okay."

"Got the signal thing?" Jenny asked Chris nervously. "You'll have to use it. I'm scared."

Before Chris could reply, Alston came to a neat stop behind the truck.

A sudden awful thought struck Chris. What if Alston kept driving around the circle? It was much too close to the fire for safety. "Jenny, we have to tell him what we're going to do," he hurriedly whispered. "Alston's the only nice guy around here."

"Okay. You tell him. And you'd both better get away from the front doors, too. Get those flares going! See you later!" She hopped out of the car. "Thanks, Alston. And when I say 'go,' you bump. Okay?"

Alston nodded.

Jenny raced around and jumped into the driver's seat of the truck. She released the brake and stuck her arm out the window.

"Okay, Alston. Bump," Chris said, his heart crowding into his throat as he watched Jenny's signal wave. "And *she*'s scared! Man! I should never have let her get in that truck," he said aloud.

At that moment, Alston bumped, and before Chris's horrified eyes the truck, with Jenny in it, was gathering speed and heading for the straight-away — and the fire.

"Jenny steer truck into fire?" Alston asked curiously. "Then jump?"

Chris suddenly remembered his own job — to send up the flares. "Drive up past the house," he choked, "then *stop*. Be sure to *stop!*"

"Okay," Alston agreed. "But see Jenny jump first."

Chris's heart was in his mouth by the time the truck containing Jenny turned into the straight-away. "Jump, Jenny, *jump!*" he begged aloud.

In the light of the flames, they saw the truck door open, and Jenny's wild leap just before the truck moved on slowly but steadily into the pile of burning wood. Jenny raced for dear life back toward the house.

"Good!" Alston said. He looked at Chris. "Don't like," he added, pointing toward the truck.

"Get *going*, Alston. Please!"

Beyond the house, Alston brought the car to a stop. "Let you out?"

With trembling fingers, Chris opened the metal

box, drew out the flare pistol, and fitted in a cartridge. "Now, you stay RIGHT HERE," he said to Alston. "We're going to have — have fireworks. Watch. Okay?"

He leaped from the car. I hope that got across, he thought frantically and swung his arm upward. Closing his eyes tight, he squeezed the trigger. There was a hissing, swishing sound. "At least I didn't put it in backward," he breathed. Then came Jenny's voice, right beside him, and he'd never been happier to hear it.

"Oh, Chris! You're *wonderful*! Look!"

"*I'm* wonderful!" Chris opened his eyes. High above them a parachute flare swung lazily, turning the sky, the earth, and the sea beyond into a rosy glow.

"Keep them going!" Jenny shouted.

Chris reached for a second cartridge, reloaded, and fired. This time a beautiful starburst of light went hissing up into the pink sky.

"We're in business!" he cried.

"Two gone and eight to go!" Jenny jumped up and down.

Chris lifted his arm for the third time, but before he could pull the trigger, there was a tremendous explosion from the barricade. Blast after blast sent huge pieces of the truck high in the air.

"Dynamite!" Chris shouted.

"It must have been in the truck," Jenny shouted back.

Chris looked at her. "Honestly, Jenny. You say the brightest things."

Jenny clutched his arm. "Look! Here they come!"

Fake Cliff, his sister, and Monty rushed out into the front drive.

Maybe it was the sight of his stern brother and sister, or the brilliant sky, or the blasts, or the roaring blaze — anyway, it was all too much for Alston. With a roar of the engine and a spurt of gravel, he took off in the big car, leaving Jenny and Chris staring after him in horror.

Around and around the circle he tore, making racing turns that churned up gravel and drove the three in the driveway back to the house.

"Man!" Chris gasped. "This is like the Indy!"

13

Jenny and Chris were awestruck by the sight they had created — flares floating in the sky, comet lights whizzing, flames crackling and roaring from the drive. And now Alston's wild looping race was turning Cliffspray's dignified circular drive into a miniature Indianapolis Speedway.

Shouts came from the front entrance, but the vain commands failed to stop Alston.

"I wish Jim and Emily could see this!" Chris exclaimed excitedly.

Jim and Emily! Jenny gasped. Now was *really* the time to act. "Chris! We've got to get them. *They're* the ones tied up now."

She thought rapidly. "Look, you keep on with the fireworks and I'll try to get in by the back door."

Chris reloaded and sent another starburst up into the sky. "Okay. And I'll keep moving around just in case Alston runs out of gas. They'd nab me fast if that happened."

In the near-daylight of the flares, Jenny raced along by the granite-sided old mansion. As she made a skidding turn at the back corner, the pound of waves beating and foaming on the rocks below the nearby cliff edge came to her ears.

It was easy to find the back door, but Jenny's heart sank as she tried the knob. Locked. And the first floor windows were too high to be reached from the ground. "What can I *do?*" she moaned. "I've *got* to get in."

At that moment, one of Chris's parachute flares went floating seaward. As the light on the ocean side grew even brighter, Jenny spied the dim, dark basement windows. They seemed to crouch above the ground — dark entrances into the earth itself.

Jenny dropped to her knees and tried to peer in. The glass, grimy with years of dirt and salt spray, obscured her view.

Hurriedly she began searching for something to use for smashing the panes. "This ought to do it," she muttered, picking up a good-sized rock. "Now which window should I smash? I'd sure hate to drop into a locked room. They'd *never* find me."

Her thoughts churned. "Maybe I can find the real Dr. Cliff's window. I could tell him, 'Help is coming.' "

Her words made her shiver. *Was* help coming? "We haven't heard one fire engine siren yet," she muttered. Wouldn't there be a fire department some place between Cliffspray and Alston? Wouldn't *somebody* have called the police by now? *What if everybody for miles around thinks the lights and explosions are only a Labor Day weekend celebration?"*

For a moment, Jenny stood stock still, horror on her face. "It's *really* up to me. I'll get upstairs even if it means falling into Fake Cliff's chamber of horrors!"

And wasting no more time, Jenny pounded the rock on the nearest window.

There was enough light from the sky to at least dimly reveal the room below. It was about seven or eight feet to the floor, with nothing for her to climb down on.

Jenny went on to the next window. She heaved the rock forward. This time glass shattered, but no open space came in view. "It's the experiment room," Jenny whispered to herself. "Naturally they'd have it boarded up. But I could be sure to get upstairs from there if I can just get *down*."

Frantically, she began pounding the boarding close to the window frame, and before long she heard the screech of loosening nails and caught a glimpse of bright light beyond. One more *thwack* and the boarding tumbled to the floor below.

Almost dreading the sight that might meet her eyes, Jenny peered in. Half in relief and half in disappointment, she saw no glowing tubes bubbling horrible shades of green and amber. No terrible throbbing thing lay stretched out on a table with electric wires attached to it. Instead, there were only boxes and boxes neatly stacked and some kind of heavy, flat-looking kind of machine.

Jenny drew a deep breath of relief. But how to get down? She looked along either side of the walls — and saw a rusty old pipe along one side of the window.

Carefully, she reached out for its cold, rough surface. Clenching the pipe, Jenny swung head-first into the room, clung for a moment to get an ankle grip, then shinnied down to the floor.

She ran to the boxy-looking machine — and right away she knew what was in the stacked boxes.

Money!

The equipment for Fake Cliff's great experiment was nothing but a small printing press!

"Why! They're nothing but a gang of counterfeiters!" she exclaimed in disgust. "Just plain, common *criminals*!"

She spun around and ran at top speed through the open doorway and up the basement steps to the main floor.

As Jenny came blasting through the swinging door into the dining room, she saw that everyone at the table was tightly bound to the chairs.

"Jenny!" Emily gasped. "Where did you come from?"

"The basement," Jenny said coolly. "Where's a knife?"

It was no easy job sawing through the knotted strips that held Jim's wrists. The carving knife from the table was too big for the job, and Jenny had to work carefully. To the questions everyone flung at her, she said only, "Tell you later. Jim, when I get your other hand loose, you undo the ties on your ankles while I go find a paring knife. This knife's awful. We'll have to work fast. They're all out front. Maybe we can grab them."

"Is my father in the basement?" Andrea asked.

"My goodness, Andrea!" Jenny blurted out. "I don't know. I couldn't take time to look!"

She ripped through the last knot on the second strip, started for the kitchen, stopped, and turned back. "I'm sure he's safe, Andrea. Don't worry. I'll untie you next."

She came back in seconds with two paring knives, handed one to Jim, and bent down to free Andrea. And the harder she sawed away, the madder she got. "Those — those cheapskates!" she muttered. "All ready to cheat the world and so mean they'd do anything just so nobody would find out about their miserable *experiment*. And I bet they've been awfully mean to poor old Alston, too. He doesn't like any of them or he'd have stopped Chris and me instead of helping us. *Phooey* to them!" she exploded.

"Phooey who?" Emily asked. "Jenny, what are you mumbling about?"

Jenny made a last slash and Andrea was free. "Here. Take this and untie Emily," she said, her face flushed red with anger. "I have other things to do."

Before anybody could say "what?" or "thank you," Jenny stalked out of the room and down a hall that, for the first time in many years, glowed with light from the open doors.

One big thought was in Jenny's head. *Get Monty before he, too, realizes that the people around think it's just a Labor Day celebration and that nobody's coming.*

Her heart thumped and she could hardly keep her knees steady as she headed for the front entrance.

Fake Cliff, his sister, and Monty were pressed back against the front wall of the mansion. Every whirl that Alston made seemed to come closer to the edge of the front steps.

"He's going to kill us!" Monty gasped. "I'm going to shoot out the tires!"

"Oh, no you're not," Jenny Blair said, calmly.

As all three spun in her direction, an amazing thing happened. The awful feeling she'd had for so many hours suddenly seemed to float away.

"You!" he exclaimed furiously.

"Me." Jenny stared coldly from Fake Cliff to Monty.

"Mr. Monty, do you wish to hand over that gun? Or do you plan to add murder to your other crimes?" She held out her hand, and it was as steady and strong as old Cliffspray itself.

"You little — "

Monty's words broke off as the wail of sirens rose above the rush of Alston's speeding spree. Fire engines, police cars, ambulances — everything on wheels seemed to be headed for Cliffspray!

Monty, the experienced criminal, started to run, dragging Jenny with him. "Come on!" he shouted to the fake Cliff.

But the fake doctor wore his most sharklike smile. "Keep your head, Monty," he said. "I'll pull us out of this, too, with everything intact. If we run, we lose all. Give her the gun. She won't use it."

Jenny took the gun, but she felt fear come flooding back.

14

The night sky was still abloom with parachute flares when the last ember of the giant bonfire had died beneath chemical spray.

Chief Perry, of the Alston Bay Volunteer Fire Brigade, signaled his men to march forward.

Axes in hand, light glowing on shiny slickers and black helmets, the fire fighters tramped over charred logs and sodden leaves. Behind them marched four state troopers in pairs, with a civilian walking between. Next came two white-clad men carrying medical bags. And behind them all shone the long headlight beams from the fire engine, the police cruisers, the ambulance, and more cars still arriving.

Alston slowed his dizzying journey and braked the big car to a stop. "Ride?" he called out cheerfully.

"What's going on here?" Chief Perry shouted angrily.

"Plenty," Alston answered.

As the state troopers, now in the lead, strode up to the entrance of Cliffspray, Fake Cliff stepped forward. "Thank goodness, officers, you've arrived! And none too soon! These *hooligans* have had us at their mercy for twenty-four dreadful hours! Another five minutes and you would have been too late." He turned to Jenny. "Hand over that weapon, young lady."

"Certainly," Jenny said politely. She stepped forward and daintily offered Monty's gun to a trooper. "I'd better call my brother. He's around here someplace."

She went to the corner of the steps. "Chri-is!"

Chris rose almost at her feet from his hiding place beneath a lilac bush.

"My goodness!" Jenny gasped. "How'd you get *there?*"

"Well, nobody was looking," Chris lifted the signal flare pistol, "so I hid just in case I had to make a last-ditch stand."

He turned to the officers. "But it isn't a weapon, so there's no need to arrest me."

"It's a dangerous toy, son. Luckily the wind was blowing them out over the sea," said the fire chief. "Flares can start bad fires. They're flaming phosphorus, you know."

From behind the solid block of state troopers, a familiar figure pushed forward. "Chris Blair, just what do you think you're doing?"

Chris's jaw dropped. "Dad! How'd *you* get here?"

"Yes, Daddy," Jenny tried to keep her voice steady — and didn't make it. "We weren't expecting you until Thursday," she sobbed.

Fake Cliff stepped straight up to Dr. Blair. "As the father of these — these *ruffians*, you'll have a great deal to account for, sir. I innocently — I may say *generously* — offered four young persons shelter from last night's storm. This, *this* is how I've been paid for my kindness."

"I'm afraid, Doctor, we'll have to detain them," a state trooper spoke up. "It looks pretty serious."

"It certainly is," boomed a voice from the doorway. A tall, silver-haired man stepped out. "I am Dr. Sterling Cliff, officer, and were it not for these children, my daughter and I would still be captives of these villains." He pointed to Monty and Fake Cliff.

Behind him, Andrea, Emily, and Jim came crowding out.

"If it weren't for Chris and Jenny, Dad," Jim said, coming down the steps, "we'd *all* be captives — or maybe worse."

He turned to the officers. "If you'll follow me, I'll show you something pretty interesting in the basement."

Miss "Cliff" and her brother seemed to shrivel. And Monty, muttering, sagged down to the steps.

It was some time before the crowd of Alston Bay villagers, their hard-working fire fighters, the ambulance, and the three counterfeiters in the grip of state troopers were gone. The remaining troopers stayed behind to stand guard over the "money," and to keep an eye on Alston.

"But you're not going to arrest him," Jenny told them firmly. "It wouldn't be fair. They've been mean to him, and I guess that's why he helped Chris and me a *lot*."

"We couldn't have managed without Alston," Chris added. "Dad, couldn't he come with us?"

Dr. Blair shook his head. "No, Chris. Afraid not. But he won't be forgotten, I promise you. Alston needs special help."

"And friends," Jenny said.

Dr. Cliff sighed. "The Simses — that's who the masqueraders and Alston really are — used to live in an old house further on. It's gone now. I played with Ronald and Alston the summer we lived here. Ronald and his sister were always mean-minded, and they led poor Alston around by the nose. My parents were kind to them, but all those two apparently remembered was that this old place would make a good hideout and that it had a foolish history of a ghost."

"Don't you believe in the Ghost of Cliffspray?" Jenny asked, wide-eyed. "Andrea said it almost killed you as a boy."

"My mother thought so. I was simply walking

in my sleep. I'm a scientist, Jenny. And I don't believe in ghosts. In fact, I named my daughter 'Andrea' to show the family how foolish it was to believe in ghosts."

"But the voice — we heard it!"

"Yes, well, I think it was a trick. Alston's grandfather was the contractor who built this house, and he was a great practical joker. The Simses have always been — well — eccentrics. Who knows? He may have planted some audio device. Anyway, he died soon after building it."

Dr. Cliff paused, then turned to Dr. Blair. "Well, sir, I don't imagine there is much you can do about the station wagon until tomorrow. If Alston has left any gas in my car, shall we all crowd in? We might get as far as Alston — the town, that is."

"We've been on our way there all day," Chris giggled. "But just one more thing, Dad. How did you get here tonight?"

Dr. Blair looked grim. "I did have a call from that rascal and agreed to come here Thursday. Then later, I changed my mind. I remembered you'd miss school opening."

Chris and Jenny grinned at each other.

"Well, what's so funny?" their father asked. "You know I believe school comes first. So I tried to call back and found there was no telephone, and the local operator insisted Cliffspray had been closed for years. That was when I called the state police and came straight here. Now let's get started.

All but Jenny turned toward the car. "Just a minute, Dr. Cliff." She hesitated. "You see I do believe in ghosts. I'm sure I heard a real one speak."

They all watched as for the last time she opened the forbidding old doors. "Good-bye, Ghost of Cliffspray," she called in a clear voice. "Good-bye!"

There was a second's silence. And, then, faint but clear, a bell-like sound came back to them all.

"Good-bye. Good-bye. Good-bye." Softly, it died away.

Dr. Cliff stared. Then in a voice so low that the Ghost of Cliffspray could never have heard, he murmured softly, "Echoes. Just echoes."

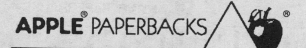